Books by Olive Moore

FICTION

Celestial Seraglio
Spleen
Fugue

NONFICTION

The Apple Is Bitten Again

OLIVE MOORE

Spleen

Dalkey Archive Press

Spleen was first published in the U.S. by Harper & Brothers in
October 1930 (as *Repentance at Leisure*) and in England by Jarrolds in
November 1930 (as *Spleen*).
Corrected text first published in Olive Moore's *Collected Writings*
(Dalkey Archive Press, 1992), pp. 109-232.

Library of Congress Cataloging-in-Publication Data
Moore, Olive.
Spleen : a novel / Olive Moore. — 1st pbk. ed.
p.   cm.
Includes bibliographical references.
I. Title.
PR6025.O575S65   1996   813'.52—dc20   96-16131
ISBN 1-56478-148-8

Dalkey Archive Press
Illinois State University
Campus Box 4241
Normal, IL 61790-4241

*Printed on permanent/durable acid-free paper and bound in the
United States of America*

and the elephant said to the flea: don't push.

G oats with long purple udders and sly drooping faces passed, trailing a strong smell of goat. She watched the woman take from her skirt a piece of bread, break a corner and give it to the child, a calm socratic child with stony eyes, and return to her business of bringing her stick down sharply across the undulating hindquarters of her goats, undulating slowly over the long Saracen road, their heavy purple udders swinging pendulously to the bleating of their neck-bells. Soon they would be far away, small dark pellets of their own dropping, the woman dwarfed to the size of the child, the child scarcely discernible, passing out under the archway to the town. As at a signal the bells of San Soccorso would give out a wild and shrill salute, rushing out on the air as a flight of famished gulls, scattering the evening mood in noise and restlessness. Six o'clock.

How well she knew it all. Morning and evening she had seen them pass, the same woman with angry pointed cries, the same stick, the same blows, possibly the same petticoats, the same children grown to grandchildren, the same goats perpetually renewing themselves, replaced, undulating, docile, the same purple udders, the same golden satyr-eye half-closed, the same acrid smell of goats passing; and twenty-two years had made it hardly more real to her than on the morning on which, leaning out on the ship's rail, her eyes set to the horizon, she had seen the island lying in glittering staccato relief on its sea-bed of plumed green, the crisp blue-green of early maize. She had looked down at the fishermen's boats come to fetch the passengers and their goods and had seen a vast tangle of heaving reeds under their covering of light sea, the marbled floor of the sea from which Foria rose, and it had seemed to her like the surprised dark suspicious stares at herself, at her wedding ring, at her sole companion the round young peasant woman from Piacenza carrying her baby, which she had endured these three weary days. And then back again and up at Foria, crowned by Mont' Epomana its tip still lost in the morning clouds, its colour-streaked waterfront heaped like the bright scrapings from an artist's palette. Journey's end and the angry cries of the Piacentina refusing in the name of the Blessed Virgin, protectress of all things helpless, to jump in a boat overstacked with wine barrels and melons, and not until the child had been taken from her, leaping full strength on to the feet of the water-seller who had been prying up her petticoats.

What would dear Stephen and Stephen's father and pouter-pigeon mamma and Dora with her pale protecting eyes, lovesick, and that sullen snub-nosed girl lost among the underhousemaids who had been rescued, and Barrett who so despised hesitating inefficient orders, and the interminable procession of other hired people at Sharvells which people such as Stephen and his pouter-pigeon mamma considered necessary to the well-being and upkeep of dear Stephen and pouter-pigeons, what would they say could they see her now sitting between the Piacentina and the garlic-thick melon merchant, shirt open to the waist and black energetic hair bristling thickly down his chest; her small patent leather feet, so correct, so refinedly helpless, looking out from under the heavy folds of the blue serge skirt of her travelling costume, ample, braided, the cape coming to her elbows covered with the very latest ornamentation in shining silk, heavy, solid, expensive; the hat a masterpiece of discretion, four brims of fine straw, laced and interlaced, escaping, recaptured, poised well forward on the brow and held there by coils of hair, an elegant misshapen mass of curls and puffs leaping forward and outward from behind the ears.

What would they say to her sitting among the wine barrels and the melons and the garlic-reeking unclean foreigners, her patent leather foot nudged at intervals by the melon-merchant with the naked bristling chest?

She has gone back, back to where she belongs. For the best. As I said at the beginning of this painful. I know. I know I should not say so, but I did say. And it is always a mistake to raise people from. The crimson satin walls of the dining-room and the vast curved window admitting one to the finest view in the county.

Ruth. Dearest Ruth. Dora's pale protecting eyes, lovesick. Do not let them make you unhappy.

Madam, Barrett says. Her heart dropped down into the tangle of weeds, but it was only the Piacentina assuring her charge that he was most beautiful, beautiful.

Soft and caressing the blue air as she raised her head. She had felt all at once sick and so tired. In a few minutes the journey would be at an end, for ever. Never again to move from the niche which she had found for herself; nor answer questions.

She laid her fingers on the water as in a vaschetta d'acqua santa. It was warm. Of course, warm. Warm water, blue-shining water, radiant water, Italian water. Of course Italian water, for she was in Italy. At last and for ever, and only three days since she had sat in the waiting-room at Victoria and the boat train had seemed to be delayed for many hours only to crawl away for many hours more and no nearer France; and suddenly some-one was thrusting a brown face down into hers and shouting at her, menacing her with teeth strong, sharp and white as sea-foam.

—Sbarcate, sbarcate Signori! shrieked the face.

—Quant' è simpatica! nodded the admiring melon-merchant, staring at her delicate frightened face drooping beneath the weight of her four-brimmed hat and elegant mountain of hair. But the water-seller staring through the heavy expensive travelling costume, said he did not think she would be of much use, that meagre foreign type never was, and spat out something that put the men in an uproar and set the Piacentina's face on fire.

—Sbarcate, sbarcate Signori! shrieked the face again, and now thrust out a long gnarled branch of an arm and jerked her roughly to her feet. And Ruth who did not want this arm had found herself clinging to it despairingly. She was tired sick and giddy with sudden fear. How they had frightened her that first morning! The sudden rough jerking to her feet had come as a blow across the face. All that had been warm and blue had turned heavy and menacing. What would become of her she had wondered foolishly if she disobeyed? Beneath her the small boat swayed and beat the water, the hot intense sand blazed up in to her eyes as she stood swaying idiotically with the boat and clutching heavily at the neapolitan's arm, like some-one blind caught in a panicking crowd.

She had been aware of rows of brown faces and foaming teeth gathering on the jetty and hemming her in, leagued against her with this savage to whose arm she was hanging. If she moved she would step into the very midst of their shouts; then she must stay where she was for fear of treading on a grinning mouth with a voice shrieking out of it like an evil flame. The shouts grew louder. The neapolitan's face came down close to hers and out of the mouth came the shrill snapping of a thousand twigs about her ears. Quickly she pulled her head away, but held on, held on with her feet pressed tightly together and swaying to the nightmare rhythm of the boat. All at once a black spot dissolved and blotted out the other detached black spots and was standing by itself on the swaying sands calling to the face itself, and the face was calling back, beating the twigs about her head and eyes. The sky fell beneath her feet, a thick glittering canopy of sand swung above her head and with it mouths, dark heads, sounds, shook, dissolved, flashed by and swung back again and up and back again and up. Her eyes closed, drowning in heat and terror. She was swung up suddenly and the sands passed away beneath her and she was carried nearer to the detached blot. The sounds it made were quite different from the sounds she had been afraid to step on. They were soft, reassuring sounds; gentle, caressing sounds; restful as hands trailing in cold water. Cool, cool, cool, and kingcups, and cool beads of water on grass, lush, tangled grass, odorous earth-hair to lay a forehead on. Such had been her first and vague impression of Donna Lisetta, and in all the twenty-two years of her life on this strange dark-hearted island, it had remained and strengthened. The sound of the voice calmed the panic that possessed her, and she saw that the sands were passing away under her because the neapolitan was running across them with her in his arms, and out on to the stones of the little port where he placed her in a carriage with an awning and a tasselled horse. Placed her gently and with a smile, nodding; his teeth in his lean dark face showing strong, sharp and white as sea-foam.

Beside her on the empty seat they wanted to put the Piacentina and the baby. No. O no. She waved them away with a feeble hand. No. She looked around her helplessly as though making her way through a fog. She wanted the blot, the voice, the cool woman with the cool green voice that had calmed her panic.

This made no favourable impression on the italians. A young mother and waving away her own child? It could not be. The Piacentina and the baby were pressed forward again; actually her foot was on the carriage step. But again Ruth waved them feebly away; even going so far as to put out a weak hand and give a feathery brush which was meant to be a strong push to the Piacentina's shoulder, pushing her away, far away and out of sight and into the sea if necessary.

The Piacentina got down and looked with round astonished into round astonished eyes. They were saying something. They were going to start shouting again and beating her over the face and eyes with shrill crackling twigs. Her head rolled feebly on her neck; it was growing heavy again and out of control. She began to cry drearily, unable to control the hiccoughing of her sobs. She wanted to dissolve completely away in the tears pouring over her cheeks.

Here was a singular treat for the Forians. Not since Giachino's woman had run into the piazza with her head cracked from eye to jaw and the blood making a pool sufficient to bathe an infant in, had there been so much to gape at. Indeed there had never been so much. What more common, after all, than to see one of their womenfolk with slit jaws, or more rare than an elegant foreign lady, a lady of evident distinction and richly dressed, blubbering like a sick child under their hundred eyes? And the elegant foreign lady would have sat there all day and blubbered while they stood around and watched her, had not Lisetta rescued her again, climbing to the empty seat and taking charge of her head by resting it on her shoulder.

—E stanca, la poverina, said Donna Lisetta to the staring eyes. Stanca, that meant tired. The first word she had understood for so long. Yes, yes, yes. Si. I am tired. I am stanca, si. Stanca. I am tired. But she was safe. She wanted to tell them to put the Piacentina in a carriage too. But she couldn't. She hadn't the strength. And besides she no longer cared. Let her find one for herself. Or let her walk.

They swung round and up a narrow side street, out on the miniature tree-bordered piazza, through more narrow streets and more turnings, under a crumbling fern-covered archway and out on the long straight road leading away from the town. She had seen nothing but the hot powdery road rolling away beneath her, and that imperfectly and through a mist. The unaccustomed heat, the yellow glare, the dust, were as a blanket held gently but persistently over her face and head. She submitted to it and fell soundly asleep on Donna Lisetta's strong black-silk bosom.

They carried her to her room and left her sleeping. They hesitated to leave her, the three women who had seen to her undressing. Looking down at the pale soft face on its pillow of coarse hand-woven linen they felt her to be altogether too fragile, too docile, and entirely helpless. But they were quite wrong. For all her endearing gentle appearance she was not a little mad, quite capable, and very determined.

A thin howl, drawn out and ending abruptly in a shriek, startled the air. The evening steamer from Naples came round the bend of the porto, conveying its awareness of its importance in the evening life of the island; all the very blue water to itself. It was always the first to break up the evening peace getting in its noise before San Soccorso which had to wait the hour but scored in a ten-minute vengeful display of farmyard cackling.

There was a sudden kindling of movement on the goat road; road which, legacy of Saracen conquerors twelve hundred years since, the Forian traitors to this early blood ridiculously called Via dei Angeli. Absurd as the crosses and campanili attached to the humped and tiled mosques and remnant walls of pagan temples scattered in profusion over the island.

The road was busy at this hour. Human caryatids moved over it, crested, placing their feet swiftly and surely in a nereid-swing of the hips, their long dark petticoats beating about their ankles. Monumental, eternal, these women as they swung past with rhythmic tread, the red clay jars motionless on their firm heads. In single file whole families moved along, graded from the tallest in front to the one not more than five years old, her miniature jar tilted perilously on her little head but more often hugged safely in her arms. The women's hour.

When the boat has passed on to Castoli its next stop on the island, the road would be broken-up in a clattering of hoofs, in the ai ah ahs of raucous donkey boys, blows, angry sounds, the thudding of bare feet, cart wheels grinding, the crack of swirling whips. Men and boys returning from the port with barrels of wine and oil, the huge piled baskets of scarlet tomatoes, the ice in the long plaited sacks which they plaited themselves and sold in Naples. Dark and wiry, they ran shouting about the road beside their beasts, beating them, cursing them, urging them, leaping ahead and leaping back again, as though they were the last of a victorious army homing in triumph with their loot of conqueror's gold. And they did this morning and evening with the same unquenchable vitality and noise, the arrival of the Naples boat transforming them from dark silent effaced creatures into this torrential outpouring of masculine energy, ravaging them, driving them angrily unsparingly as they drove their beasts.

But the crested women with nereid-swinging hips moved in their slow-measured step, monumental, eternal. They were going to the wells and fountains of the town to fetch water. In the morning before the sun was at its height and in the evening when it was spent, they moved over the Saracen road to fetch the water, evenly, calmly. Unlike the men it evoked in them no sense of triumph so that they brought no battle-fever, no heroics, no mock-splendour to the doing of an everyday task. So much the worse for them, she had always thought. For their reward their half-hour of shrill clatter at the well, water-jars swung to their head cushions, and back again, nereid-swinging, calm, eternal, empty and joyless.

She too could carry a water jar on her head, the fine english signora; though having found that it was not as difficult as she had supposed she had long ceased doing it. Secretly she had lowered herself in their esteem; though not secretly for she knew it well enough and who, after all?, can keep respect for twenty-two years because of an arrival in an elegant travelling costume with braided cape and exquisite pointed shoes. Too much mystery for respect, thought the islanders. No letters. No visits. No family, then. Ah-ah these cold foreign women who look one steadily in the face and make no distinction in their talk. Men in petticoats, poor godless creatures. But Ruth had found her niche and was never again to explain herself away to anyone but herself, and had even ceased to do that for a very long time now.

Strange that in twenty-two years her environment and existence should have become scarcely more real to her. But she had never belonged, although at first young, eager, she had tried. She waited. She seemed to be resting there; a stage on a journey she was not conscious of desiring to complete. Ruth herself was unable to understand how, entering as she did into the heart of the place and its people, she was yet unable to make them hers. Her days had passed in caryatid calm, empty, joyless, undeviating, as she had willed. For always she was fair. She never forgot it was of her own choosing. That she had thrust herself on them, had insisted on their having her, years before foreigners were heard of on the island.

Now of course they were fairly common. The Naples passenger boat that once had called weekly, now called twice a day, and on Sundays there were crowded excursion boats bringing the neapolitans to bathe and picnic. White stark hotels were being conjured up, and the townspeople let rooms all through the summer and autumn months and were growing rich and impudent on it. In Naples one day she had been startled by the sight of a large garish poster in a Tourist Agency window. Foria had been promoted to Agency patronage. Entering she was supplied with an illustrated booklet and dates and times and guide services. True, Foria had no Blue Grotto as had its prosperous neighbour, but it had been no less the pleasure ground of Rome's wealthy and notorious; and Horace himself gazing out from the Bay of Baia (at the island said the booklet) had proclaimed it the loveliest sight in the world. The Agency now having cast a belated eye in the same direction seemed grateful to Horace for this remark; it received an entire page to itself.

On her way home, waiting at Baia for the steamer, she had searched the horizon for Foria, yet although the evening was of that limpid vibrating kind in which one reaches out a hand to touch objects many miles distant, and although she could see plainly the menacing twin humps of Capri and the rounded Procida, she could not see the particular island which, in the Agency booklet, Horace had had in mind when praising the loveliness of the Bay. Unless his eyesight was finer than mine, she reflected, which I doubt. All of which meant that the island was attracting the attention of the mainland, and that the attention of the mainland as the stark white hotels showed, was worth attracting.

But Ruth knew a time when children ran behind their mothers' skirts at the sight of her, and could not be coaxed away until she had passed. And she had liked it enormously the fierce shyness of the children and the morose savage shyness of their elders. Silent indifferent dark-hearted people. At first (she could now laugh at that early fear) they had seemed altogether sinister and hostile to her. It was so unlike anything she had ever known and herself so very much in their power. But she had liked their self-contained impertinence, their complete absence or understanding of respect or deference. Once beyond her first and physical fear of them she had liked at once these people who rarely talked. At first she had thought they sat about silently because, not being able to understand them, it was useless to address her. But not a bit of it. They spoke rarely because they had rarely a desire to speak. And Ruth coming from a world where talk if not spontaneous must be induced and where the larynx was the most productive part of the human body, loved and marvelled at these people for their silences. Twenty-two years remained an unreality; but she had been grateful for the silence. She was her sole companion. I am, she quoted Donne, the self-consumer of my woes; and was glad that her years had not been spent in the wetting of other people's shoulders in attitudes of varying despair.

Not a little mad and very determined the englishwoman who was never seen to handle her own child, but gave it to others to wash and feed and showed distaste when they caressed it. The Piacentina left a week after their arrival, and besides her wages Ruth gave her more than half her wardrobe; all the pretty elegant clothes her purple-dark italian eyes coveted. I do not need them, she said, indifferent, when the girl hesitated. I shall wear what Donna Lisetta wears. But the silly girl, seizing both her hands and covering them with kisses, persisted in treating it as a sacrifice and behaved much as the beggar must have behaved on getting Saint Martin's shift. And ever since she had worn the accepted peasant dress of the island, the dark sprigged apron, the dark tucked blouse, the long dark petticoat. She wore no stockings even in winter when the Graecale swept cold and clear over the Bay; she disliked zoccoli for their dreadful clap-clapping on the stone floors, and wore instead light low-heeled shoes sent especially from Naples. She cut off her elegant mountain of hair to the neck where without effort from her part, fortunately, for she had no intention of making such effort, the ends curled up and made her look more fragile more docile than ever. A little novice, said Lisetta, watching the rigid rejection of all clothes and elegances associated with her former life; and a little angel she added when Ruth's shorn tails of hair curled like altar candles in June. Not until her early thirties did Ruth let her hair grow again and make a twist of it in the nape of her neck as the other women.

From the start Donna Lisetta accepted her new lodger without question and was immensely proud of her. She accepted also the bundle of white clothes that rarely cried and remained motionless for hours on end.

S ome-one was calling her. She answered through cupped hands winging her voice like a planing bird. Graziella, Lisetta's eldest daughter, carrying a plate of grapes came through the doors leading to the veranda alcove where Ruth lay prolonging the afternoon siesta into the early evening. Was she going to the town? asked Graziella. She was not. Because I am, and la *mamma* says I am to ask if there is anything you want there. Only the day's papers and more of that red wool for Concetta's new jersey.

At the mention of Concetta's new jersey Graziella tightened her lips and stared sideways down at the grapes. What a monkey childishness! Ruth looking at her knew very well what that grimace was intended to convey. Here was Graziella, a new bride and well into the fifth month of her first child, screwing up her face because Concetta, her fourteen-years-old sister, was to have a new jersey knitted for her by the Signora, and not only a new jersey, bitterly, but a red one. Stupid and ridiculous creature! But a splendid thing from the polished obsidian head on the strong neck set well back and emphasised through years of water carrying to the narrow naked feet, dusty and just now none too clean. Pomona sulking, Artemis tamed and fertile in the name of the Father, Son, and Holy Ghost.

—When I go to Naples on Thursday, Graziella, said Ruth slowly as one enunciates to a stubborn child, I shall bring you back a thick coat, long, with a good warm collar, because it will be cold very soon and we must see that you are kept warm and happy now. (Why was she always going out of her way like this to propitiate these childish dark-hearted people to whom she was less than nothing, and must go on for ever being less than nothing no matter what she did, because the only tie they understood, the blood-tie, was not there?)

Immediate smiles, stammers, ecstatic gratitude, and the Blessed Virgin invoked and thanked personally, dear protectress of all things small. But. But. How should she say it? The Signora must not think her ungrateful. The Signora must not think she could refuse so great and desirable a gift. But. But. You do not want a coat? O yes. Indeed yes, Graziella wanted a coat; wanted a coat more than anything in the world except. Except? Except a silver offering Signora? Afterwards? Perhaps Signora? O, the offering! But you will get that in any case. Surely (gently), you knew that, Graziella? (Of course she knew it, confirmed that Madonna-monkey look that creeps slyly into such eyes in unguarded moments.) That would be seen to in Naples as well, but later much later. More smiles, more stammers, more gratitude to the Blessed Virgin and herself sitting jointly hand in hand; and Ruth was left to her evening solitude again.

Three years after she came to the island she had placed a silver plaque for Graziella, a smiling cherub head addressed and dated, in the Church of Monte Vergine to thank the mountain goddess for Lisetta's safe delivery; and another for Concetta when her turn came. How grateful Lisetta had been! for she was on the point of offering up her best white coral earrings which, returning them hastily to their little box, the Virgin could not have liked nearly as much. For now both Graziella and Concetta were represented in Heaven by images such as old Celestino with the engraved silver heart which he had offered up thirty years ago for the cure of his left arm (hearts being nearly five lire cheaper than arms) and which he had never ceased to boast about, could bite his fingers at.

And already it was Graziella's turn. A sense of pleased wonder came over Ruth as she took in the import of this thing which she had known from the start and but now realised. She anticipated her next trip to Naples; saw herself once again chosing, suggesting, harassing the silversmith with requests for a doric simplicity whilst fingering the most choice examples of his perplexed and tortuous baroque. Dear strange adopted people! After all she had made them hers, and she liked them the better for never completely accepting her.

She leaned forward to watch Graziella below pass swiftly sinuously between the vines. Already the rise under her sprigged cotton apron was well-defined. Balanced against the rigid set of the girl's smooth head it seemed to urge her forward in a victorious sweep, as though she continually pushed aside an invisible obstacle and the conquered path unwound itself before her proud feet.

L eaning forward to watch her from sight Ruth thought: where she treads flowers should spring. And she waited a little breathlessly for the earth to respond, to give a sign, to welcome fecundity as Ceres passed. To break up gladly in a ribbon of buttercups. Set a thousand birds to sing. Leave a primrose in each footprint. Instinctively she still turned to meadow-flowers and grass in this grass-parched birdless land. But Ceres passed with her hot dusty feet unheralded, between the dusty vines, along the hot dusty road, a small grey cloud of dust pursuing her heels to the town.

—Yet there should be flowers! she thought foolishly, almost passionately, as though the earth had nothing more urgent to do than break in coloured flames around the feet of pregnant young females off to gossip at the public fountains. Yet not so foolish seeing that it had done so once. Once when Botticelli's miraculously burdened women had passed the earth had answered and caressed their narrow feet. Once, but not again. Not that one believed; not that for a moment one believed that Sandro's Graces could produce anything more real than doves, or singing birds, or cherub heads for the rapturous upholding of celestial feet. Or that his Spring winging divinely across canvas had done more than break in the load of flowers her long fingers were scattering.

Not that one believed, but that one wanted to believe. The hand turning the pages of her book trembled. She ought not to let her mind pursue the subject; and she knew by her quickened heart-beats that it was now too late to withdraw again into her trained impersonality.

Graziella was not afraid; not in the least afraid. These women knew no fear. At most a faint superstitious dread that after its birth the child might be taken from them to live in Paradise, the little innocent. But who would grudge, as she had once been horrified to hear Padre Antonio explain, who would grudge Our Lady such a gift: She whose mother-heart had been left torn and bleeding?

And scarcely any pain at all. Like the gypsy or nomad women kneeling behind a hedge, exerting themselves, picking it up, wrapping it round, and starting after the caravans moving unconcernedly away. Nothing at all. One day she would return from the beach or from the town with the day's papers, and Lisetta would run out to her with a face of beatitude announcing that Graziella had been delivered of whatever she had had to deliver, and Graziella, completed, would be sitting up in bed, the sweat still on her smiling face, accepting the cup of zabaglione and the figs, and the next day she would be up and about, singing to her infant, feeding it, washing it, ravished with delight in it, and binding it in the mummy-bands of a della Robbia holy child until only its face, surprised and formless, was visible. And from first to last no fear, no despair, no mental torture. Nothing that was known to colder northern women, over-civilised, over-sensitised, bearing their children in an agony of pain and bewilderment.

Her lips quivered uncontrollably. To steady herself she leaned against the pillows of her chair and stared over the blue shining water of the Bay to where, on the horizon, the evening sky prepared for an Ascension. Only to find the tears pouring down her cheeks and that she was crying silently. Who hadn't cried for so many years now! All the tumult and frustration hidden for so long in the background of her mind, denied, ignored, refused a hearing, lain suppressed and fermenting, seemed to be pouring out over her face as she stared at the piled clouds coming up over the edge of the Bay. How unprepared, how defenceless she felt before the suddenness of the attack!

Was it possible that because a girl with her apron jutting out in front of her passed through a vineyard, twenty-two years must melt away like a pear-drop on a child's tongue?

Plaintively and helplessly impatient her voice came to her again over the years. *But you see I do not care for men, Dora. I do not care for women. Why can one not have something else, something different, something new, something more worth having if one has to go through all this?*

She said it to Dora because she knew of no one else who would even try to understand, and because Dora loved her and being a woman could not dismiss and pooh-pooh-my-dear everything she said as the natural hysteria and lack of mental balance usual in pregnant women. Not that she was altogether fond of such dog-like devotion. Ruth liked clear decisive people. But talking to Dora was like talking aloud; and she had never talked to Stephen who was so evidently proud of her just now.

One morning on opening her eyes she was awake as though she had not slept; and she knew instantly, as though she had said her thoughts aloud, that there was but one person in the whole house to whom she wanted to speak or listen, and that this was the sullen snub-nosed girl lost among the underhousemaids, who had been rescued and had now had more than a year in which to be grateful to little Mrs Philmore the vicar's earthly comfort, creator and organiser of the local Ladies Needlework Guild with its many divisions, subdivisions, charitable activities and interferences. Sarah. Sarah Minchin. She wanted to talk with Sarah Minchin. But it was obvious that Ruth being who she was and Sarah being what she was, not even the morbid desires of pregnancy could make it possible for them to meet as equals. Apart from the tongue-tied embarrassment Sarah would experience if her lady who was not such a very real lady at all if only poor Sarah knew, plucking with young anxious fingers at the embroideries on her dressing-gown should say: Tell me, Sarah, is it true that you tried to kill yourself? You were frightened? You were angry? Tell me, Sarah. Because I too am frightened. I too am angry. Do other women feel about this as I feel?

To which Sarah had she not been well-versed in the abject and resentful deference of her class, apart from the tongue-tied inexpressiveness that sat upon her in a perpetual sulk, might have said many bitter and salutary things on the ease of protected motherhood. Even so the disgraced and retrieved Sarah could have said nothing which in her heart Ruth did not know, or had not recapitulated many times to self-aggravate her misery and confusion. Why am I not thankful? Why, why should I mind? I have always liked children; and children have always liked me. But she did mind; and the incredible thing was that it sometimes seemed to her that something outside herself minded even more than she did.

At first she could not believe it even though her face had that momentarily pinched grey look which is the first outward sign of pregnancy, and morning nausea was frequent. But when there could be no possible doubt as to what was the matter with her, Ruth was shocked, herself, at the horror that came over her. Why? Why should I mind? There was no answer. She was like a woman possessed. She was a woman possessed; and she was horrified at the possession of herself by this thing she neither understood nor desired. And yet in her despair her rational self could stand aside bewildered and appalled by the horror that possessed her; as though a part of her were trying to remain aloof and sane in the midst of acting a nightmare.

Perhaps it was the indelicacy of noticing such things that kept Stephen from seeing her as anything but grey-faced and preoccupied, which would take its course; but for all the cunning of her heightened sensibilities to protect herself, Ruth could not protect herself from Dora; and yet Dora who loved her and as a woman should have tried to understand, was not a little shocked at what she guessed and almost surprised. For Dora was one of those women who for all their contempt of men and marriage are passionately fond of children and would make splendid mothers were there any known means of making them such. Yet more shocked than hurt, so awful was it to her to see her idolised Ruth's strained and frightened face, and to surprise her with eyes red from secret crying. Who would have suspected, thought the anxious Dora, that all this lay buried under Ruth's gentle detachment, under the dear eagerness which one could not help loving her for, and instantly. And all for something which should have glorified her and which Dora had always imagined she would accept calmly and gladly, and not with revulsion and a face like a tragic mask, except for the mouth which was contracted and nervous.

The unhappy Dora watching her move restlessly about the room misunderstood it all completely.

—Dearest you must not believe it as unpleasant as is supposed. The pain is over very soon. And they say that afterwards women forget their pain no matter how intense it has been at the time. That is nature's compensation.

—Pain? echoed Ruth startled, standing quite still and looking at her with a stupid dazed look on her pale face. Pain? But I have no fear of pain, Dora. Not pain. Why should you say that?

Which saved her from explaining, for what is there to explain to one who thought of birth in terms of physical pain?, that were her child presented to her in her sleep, as it were, painless, immediate, she still would not want it. And that that was exactly the reason of her fear: that she did not want her child. Dora she knew would have done her best to say what was becoming to the occasion. This was a phase which must pass. Many women must say much the same thing faced with the coming of their first child. At which she could have cried for infinite relief. Only to know that the answer to that is: until the child comes, and then the mother loves it. She must. It is nature.

Then she was wise to keep her thoughts to herself; for in her case it did not seem to be nature, even though to persuade herself she would repeat, the water-drop wearing away the stone: when it comes. Lame comfort. She knew otherwise. She was not of those who can question and answer to their advantage. Nor fearing the answer could she refrain from questioning. At night how plausible they became these inner pleadings by which she explained and condoned herself to herself, to her immediate surroundings. But as each new day which was to herald and accept the decisions of the night became but a restless wait for a return to the sheltering isolation of the night, back to the tortuous self-persuasion which the day would have nothing of, she seemed to herself the evil queen of the tales of her childhood returning at midnight to her witchcraft.

For how can one love a thing one does not desire? Perhaps because it is usual to love one's child. Then I am not usual. (How easy to accept this in the darkness of the night when the unreal becomes the obvious!) Because she knew that not wanting the child now she would not want it later. She knew it was not possible to her to love a thing she did not know or had not seen. How can one? Yet I am expected to. All women do. I am a woman. Therefore I do. And if I do not? (And at a movement real or imaginary within her.) When I breathe, it breathes. When I feed, it feeds also. Against my will. Yet when it had finished using her for its own purpose, she must welcome it and say that it was hers and that therefore she loved it (all women do) at once and without question. When it had had nothing to do with her from start to finish.

—Yet creation, Ruth, is a wonderful thing, had said Dora yesterday, hoping, looking vaguely helpful and helpfully vague.

—Is it? she questioned of the darkness, although at the time she had smiled submissively enough to please, for she knew better than to trust her secret perplexities to friendly but unfollowing minds. Is it? Do you believe that? Or are you repeating what we have all been taught and taught not to question. (After all, considered Ruth not without bitterness, what had been her friends' efforts to comfort her? It is a phase. It is nature. It is a wonderful thing.)

But I want to know what is the use of it all. Can you not try to understand me, Dora? She did not want the stories that calm frightened children. She wanted to know why the child is frightened. To what purpose: to what end? Why do I alone not feel this need? Why do I question where others accept? Why should I shrink from what others welcome? At first in her first terror of herself she had answered: because I am wicked; because I am sinful. But that got one no further than Dora's remarks, and was even more childish.

Perhaps could they see into my heart they would be more afraid even than I am. What to them is such a wonderful thing is to me fuss and ugliness. Ugliness, she thought, refusing to take back the word. And meaningless, too, and dull and hopeless. And knowing that, I am afraid. And they know that I am afraid, and they cannot answer me, but float up to gaze at me, like goldfish in a bowl. (A goldfish, she thought, whose pale evaporating eyes were meant to stare through fishy water and come to the rim of the bowl for a long aching look.) All women do. I am a woman. Therefore I must. To what purpose? If I dared ask them that! It will be like Stephen. And what will be the use of that? Or it will be like me. And what will be the use of that? But I am not to ask the reason because women have ignored the question, smiled, turned aside and talked of love. She tried and could not. Perhaps because she had known too little about love; so that she had no such consolation. (There was no bitterness in the thought. She had known it from the moment they had sent for her after the weeks of separation and she had seen his dear wasted face trying to convey his recognition of her as she had stared down at his bush of snowy beard. Turned all white of a morning, said the bony creature privileged to watch over him, still amazed and incredulous. Why was I not told? cried Ruth, cheated of a part of him.) It must be that she had no maternal sense. None whatsoever. And they regard me as something unnatural and not sane, and they may be right. A woman is expected to have a maternal sense as she is expected to have other womanly attributes. Had I been born blind or deaf they would not expect me to see or hear; that they could understand. A boy is born. Or a girl. A boy. A girl. And you know before hand every possibility of its life, and like a litany the answer is unalterable and as assured. Birth. Adolescence. Marriage. Birth. Old Age. Death.

She paused as though to make sure that it was she who had formed the words: then in the silence she repeated them. Birth. Adolescence. Marriage. Birth. Old Age. Death. That then was their wonderful thing! One had but to wait, one's mind in revolt against one's body, knowing the end and fearing it, and then because it is called nature and because one is told that one must because everyone does, one is to accept blindly what one has resented actively every moment of every day for weeks and months.

She saw it more clearly now, their wonderful thing. Some sudden turning her groping mole-mind had taken and there it was, clear as the daylight that must break upon the room when the great curtains were swung back on their heavy ropes. But the discovery, like the daylight, proved more revealing than comforting. For how does one accept the inevitable?

Because a reason had to be found for the sudden and bewildering revulsion which had taken possession of her like some deadly disease, a form of emotional galloping consumption that ravished her physically and mentally, she remembered the story her father had told her in the heavy brown workroom, untidy, serious, personal, dusty with books and smoke, worked-footstools and large humped chairs with the stuffing falling out of them, and the vast carved oak table heaped with examination papers, textbooks, blue copybooks with names sprawled over them in young difficult boyish handwriting. That had been her first emotional experience of real consequence, but she had shared it with her father whom she loved; and this time she bore it alone and it was nearer and more real to her than anything had ever been or, she felt, could be again.

It was considerable part of the solution. One is not suddenly transformed from a negatively peaceful person into a restless fury without cause; and as though to make amends for the pain she was causing her these days, she said it to Dora one afternoon as they sat together gazing out at tulip beds arranged with stiff and formidable precision and colour-graded with monotonous regard for formal landscape harmony, and none whatever for Spring itself.

—My mother, dearest, never wanted me. She found herself saying it without difficulty or shame, talking rather as people talk in their sleep but fully conscious of what they are saying, and prepared to argue it.

Never wanted her! No, and not only had not wanted her but had dreaded the very thought of her and had tried to end it all and could not and with the shock had died and she had been born barely at her seventh month. My father suffered most. It was he who had told her about it, which was brave of him for she need not have known. As the mere thought of him could set her pulse dancing, she smiled as she spoke.

Dora's face was set and unsmiling. What then would she think of me, wondered Ruth keeping her eyes on the formal travesty of Spring, who can find no reason? She had had such good cause to dread the coming of her child. (How one must beg the world's pardon with adequate reasons!) A very sound reason, not a wild intangible reason such as mine, but one real to her and terrible. (Or merely obvious?)

—You see, said Ruth slowly, my mother. My mother was not married to my father. Perhaps that, hazarded Ruth.

(But she said nothing of the handsome girl in the sombre grey fishing village near Portloe, strong-breasted, determined, a large enamel brooch at her throat, and narrow intense eyes that stared from the faded photograph in the carved frame above her father's desk, and made her small daughter's heart beat wildly each time she opened the door and watched them follow her across the room.)

Not that Dora wanted to hear more. She understood that after all these years she had overheard Ruth's secret. The secret of that bearded Jovian headmaster of that novel preparatory school in Hampshire, the widower with an only daughter. Overheard because inexplicably she felt it had not been meant for her, that she should not have been listening. She had been eavesdropping outside a confessional box. She had been listening to a sick person's delirium and some startling thing had been said quite mildly, as though the patient were asking for beef-tea, very weak. You see my mother was not married to my father. Gently: O you did not know that? No, not another cup thank you. Dear, dear beloved Ruth.

—What difference could that make to me? asked Dora loyally.

—But it may make a considerable difference to me, thought Ruth despairingly.

I think, Stephen, said Ruth. I think I carry my womb in my forehead.
—I quite definitely feel it here, pursued Ruth, drawing her brows sharply together and staring across at her husband perplexedly. Whereas I do not feel it here at all (and her hand touched her body). So that if you came and told me that all the time it is growing in my head I should not be in the least surprised. Not in the least. I should say: yes. How strange. I thought so too!

Some there are, she quoted to Dora, whose souls are more pregnant than their bodies. No. Socrates. And no one has ever thought of applying it to women. Why? Because the soul Dora is man's prerogative, and woman is but the eternal oven in which to bake the eternal bun. Nature's oven for nature's bun. Hundreds of thousands of buns daily in a variety of colours and only two shapes. All produced for one relentless purpose. Birth. Adolescence. Marriage. Birth. Old Age. Death.

—I think, said Ruth as she had said earlier in the day to Stephen. I think I carry my womb in my forehead. And I think that that, perhaps, is my curse.

But in her heart she refused to regard it as a curse. Alone, nothing could be more natural than her attitude. She was growing larger now, but that, as she had said about pain, meant nothing to her. She seemed unable to notice it. The pinched early look had left her very soon. For all her despair and resentment she could not prevent the warm peach-bloom of her cheek nor that look of physical radiance peculiar to women who are first loved, which nature insists on in her patients after the first few anxious weeks.

If she was in no way reconciled at least she was no longer afraid. Even at its strongest her fear had been but the temporary expression of her revulsion. Fear, for all that may be claimed for it, is more often cowardice; and in that direction at least she did not err. She had an abundance of courage both mental and physical, and a courage of a sort unusual in woman in that she accepted nothing but that which her mind had tested. She was no longer afraid, nor angry, nor bitter, but she was still in revolt and revolted (for how does one accept the inevitable?) and at times exasperated almost to frenzy by the purposelessness of it all. At first the more she had thought about it the less purpose she could find in it; and now understanding the purpose she could see no reason for it. Then back to the tragi-comedy of the squirrel cage. They won't bake buns? Let them bake cakes. And should they not want to bake even cakes? And not only not want, but refuse? If something outside one refuses: something one cannot control because one cannot fathom? Darkness. But nothing physical. Nor pain nor even death. Futility, perhaps.

One thing she would not, she could not accept: that women went through it all without question; were creatures possessed and content to have no say in the matter. Her mind centred more and more around the thought of what women could have done had they brought conscious thought to bear on what had always been dismissed as a pre-ordained and unalterable task. She found herself believing that had it been left to men centuries of creation would have produced some thing more vital, more exciting. But then men were the active and not the passive instruments of nature. Men questioned. Not from woman that despairing cry: my God what am I in Thy universe? To answer which sails unfurled, wings of birds and angels yielded their secret, the earth rose and parted, was weighed, sifted, spanned from the immensities of its roof to the treacheries of its floor, the moon stuffed in the pocket, the whole held negligently in the hollow of a hand. Man returning the apple to woman who first bade him eat of it; and woman (enclosed in her world within herself) humouring him, placing it carefully out of reach on the mantelpiece above the hearth which was her contribution to the whole, together with the tranquillity, the amorous fidelity, the kind sentimental cruelties necessary to its maintenance and security.

She suggested as much to Dora.

—This, said Dora, still patient, still trying to put some sense into her, this is what woman is made for. After all, said Dora.

—Was made for, corrected Ruth. Was made for.

And in that sentence sprung to defend her as it were from Dora's moral certainties—in that disconcerting way surface sentences have of proving discoveries, releasing their trap-doors at the back of the mind through which the speaker hurtles in the act of murmuring something detached and pleasing (knows that she has lost or won, will leave and nor return, and stay because life is not taken up again after such an interval and there are the children, or will leave that very night and cheat with memories the final loneliness in which all things die, or retreat, or advance, or surrender) she knew that she was no longer alone. Was made for, she had said, more to contradict than to affirm: a sullen child's last word; and had fallen on the discovery that she was not the only woman to feel about her child as she felt. Or rather that it is not only a few unnatural and unbalanced women who feel as I feel. That is not true. They like pretending that all women are born mothers. They like pretending that because women have to be mothers, born or not. That supplies their apology; feeds the conceit that man is an individual and oblivion an illusion; satisfies the weakling's need to have been spawned by divine command and ultimately entitled to equal heritage of a flowering and boundless Paternal estate. And so they pretend that only a few strange and unnatural women have denied this truth to themselves. But that is not true. She knew that now. There had always been and there would always be many such perplexed uneasy creatures, unsure, hesitating, bearing maternity with an ill grace and as something strange and outside themselves. Only their opinion was never asked or heeded. And it all began, thought Ruth idiotically, it all began when we gave up eating grass.

She was none the less convinced that she was being cheated; was being made use of against her will; was being hourly thwarted. She had the illusion that all these mental questionings, the denials, the whys and wherefores, bitterness and revulsions in which she had been caught since its inception, and with which she had been solely and persistently concerned, had arrested the action of her body; as though this thing was not to be until a satisfactory reason could be found for its being and for her wilfulness in denying it life; as though gestation was suspended until she had prepared herself to accept its consequences.

If mentally she was calmer it was because it is psychically impossible for any emotion, no matter of what intensity, to be maintained at boiling pitch for more than a relatively short period of time. In one torrential outpouring, as it were, the emotional lava overflows and subsides within itself again. Surprised, chagrined, no mountainous upheaval commemorates the event, but a mild stewpot simmer ludicrously out of proportion to the promise of its early wrath! Ruth had, however, the very definite physical sensation of having been badly bruised. So much so that often on turning her head quickly or lifting an arm or moving a foot she felt a pain shoot through her, sharp enough to bring tears to her eyes.

And then one day in her morning bath she noticed for the first time how large she had become. She couldn't believe it. Impossible! Yet it must be true for the water refused to cover her. She lay flat. And still the water refused to cover her. She sat up. Useless. She lay down again. She turned on this side. On that. She lay back flat again, resting her head against the edge of the bath, contemplating; and had to admit. Had to admit. That it was not happening in her forehead at all, but was happening very much where it was meant to happen. That while she had been angry and despairing it was growing. It was becoming. It was happening. The eternal bun was baking in the eternal oven. And all her anger and despair had meant less than nothing to it. All her revulsion had had no effect. For answer a heavy white bubble of a tightly stretched stomach and water below lap-lapping round its sides. She put up a wet hand to her eyes.

But the tears came again, insisted on coming. On an impulse she leaned forward and made them fall in large warm drops on her heavy white bubble of a tightly stretched stomach which the water refused to cover. They fell one by one, quite large and warm, ran down the sides in smooth even rills and were lost in the water lap-lapping below. A baptism. A dirge. A funeral dirge over the unborn. Your burial service, said Ruth, wept fifty years too soon. A white bubble of a coffin and tears dropping on it like earth.

For what seemed a long time she lay back, her head against the rim of the bath, contemplating herself, and seemingly unaware that the water was becoming uncomfortably tepid and that with the cold her skin was showing drawn and mottled. Except for a quick unconscious shiver now and again, she lay without moving and with her eyes half closed, her face taking on the intense abstracted look of a sleepwalker, for she was unaware either of herself or her surroundings. She was aware only of the sudden and appalling change which had come over her and left her numb. Conversion, even a mild and imperfect conversion, is an ordeal; but when it is swift and sudden and complete, when, as it were, there is no mistaking the voice that calls from bells and blossoming apple boughs, or when, again, in the dark forest the hunted stag turns on the hunter and reveals the crucifix upheld between its antlers, it is such a complete and shocking disintegration of the human soul that few, fortunately, are called upon in a lifetime to endure it more than once. Ruth read her message in the lap-lapping of the water that seemed so far away and in the tightly stretched bubble of a stomach that still seemed to her unreal and not her own; and she understood that the search was ended. An answer had been found to her questioning. Something different, said the message. Something worth having. Something beyond and above it all, said the message. Something new.

And now after the dreary perplexity of the past months, the listlessness, the morose staring, there was an unreal and luminous quality about her as though she were possessed of an abundant and inexhaustible fount of serenity of which she alone knew the source. She was transformed; she was radiant. She was excited and very happy.

So it was true that if one asked one received. If one questioned one was answered. Woman was a witch filled with a great and terrible power over mankind. The power of life, of creation, of death. How puny then the thunder of man! Jove's toy squibs. Vulcan's toy swords. Woman's thunderbolt. Miniature gods with life and death in their hands for the dealing. Hebes. Cup-bearers of gods. Chalices in which gods were renewed and born again. And they did not know it. They denied their terrible power because they ignored it. But she was going to use her power. If I am to create, she told the eager creature in her mirror, I will create. Only of course something new. Something different. Something beyond and above it all. Something worth having. She seemed to wing across floors and paths leaving no footprints. Her face wore a smile happy and continuous and if those at whom she smiled doubted at moments that she saw them they were not altogether wrong. She saw them but she seldom noticed them.

Dr Mason may have been a very old man indeed, as she believed, but he had a certain store of wisdom and accumulated facts. True, medically it was one of the most interesting manifestations of induced and sustained hysteria during pregnancy he had ever come across. But being one of those pleasantly tyrannical old gentlemen who claim life-privileges for having assisted one into the world, a service he had performed efficiently enough for her husband, he took upon himself to condone with Stephen exceedingly and give as his private opinion that hysteria in such cases is so nearly allied to madness that it is a great pity, a great pity.

But the change was altogether too harmonious and serene for madness. Secretive, mystic, and the exaltation of power. She was drunk with the terrible knowledge of her terrible power. She took to avoiding the house a good deal and to wandering secretly in the isolated and unsought woods bordering a part of the grounds. Here she would lie for hours on the earth as though embracing it. She had not done such a thing since she was a child and it brought her immense comfort and a spiritual content, in which, as in a trance, the life around her vanished and was forgotten, leaving her alone on her patch of mossy grass among the trees. The first wood anemones lifted fresh white faces from the crisp red undigested leaves of autumn, making starry and melodious patterns which the birds echoed, hung above the downy antlers of the woods like flowers of the air.

Grass had always had an intense and spiritual significance for her. Once as a small child out walking with her father she had pointed with her blackberrying cane to a particularly wild tangle of grass and tufted clover and had said: Look father, earth's beard. All divine and noble beings she had thought had beards: God and her father, and Homer, and Michelangelo, and the lion-hunting frescoed Assyrians, and the earth. Above all, the earth. In the earth's hair you cooled your hands and laid down your face; and its potency was a healing drug that never failed. They cut off Samson's beard and cried: Samson, civilisation is upon thee! And yet she would have disliked Stephen in a beard. Stephen like civilisation was smooth and refined. Dear Stephen.

Stephen who was for ever tidying up his face and composing himself, as an old lady composes her ribbons.

A large yellow leaf running with its fellows before a sudden wind fell in her lap. Ah no, Zeus! she smiled, picking it up, throwing it, watching it leap away, and reflecting how warily one must have walked when to stoop and welcome a friendly cat or lift a half-starved cur on one's lap was to find an amorous god bestriding one or bearing one arrogantly away on perilous and uncalled-for journeys over new and discordant seas! Did anxious parents of handsome daughters, forbidding all kindness to dumb animals, tell fearful tales of the dread seducer who comes in the shape of the wounded bird and gentle treacherous garlanded bull on whose back young innocence is invited to ride? And did young innocence wander forth in the morning blue and search the gracious skies for pursued and palpitating birds, and run secretly to the river's edge in the hope that among the tangled rushes stood the shining and forbidden creature, new-garlanded and eager to be off? Of course they did! by the very frequency with which it happened to these marriageable and disobedient young women borne off in absurd and smiling attitudes to be breeders of gods and heroes.

No, she intended no replica of herself or Stephen. That would indeed be a shocking waste of her new-found and terrible power, laughed Ruth. Something new. Something quite different. Something worth having. Something beyond and above it all. Something free that would defy the dreary inevitable round of years. And she counted on her fingers, pressing them in the grass: Birth. Adolescence. Marriage. Birth. Old Age. Death.

How inadequate, how humiliating, and what a mockery!

Only this could a human being achieve, and then thrust upon him without so much as a by-your-leave or would-you-prefer? Something new, she begged of the grassy beard. Let me be the first. That after all would be but fair. She had thought first. Each day she came secretly to her grassy altar and made her prayer and prostrated herself before the earth as once the greek women had prostrated themselves before the beauty of Apollo, seeking to imprint the divine image on the life within them. Not that she needed to do this for the thought was never absent from her mind, but the ritual pleased her and added to her confidence. She made no actual demands in her prayers, which in the strict sense of the word were not prayers at all but only an aching desire which possessed her utterly and made, as it were, its own demands. There was nothing shaped or definite about her plea. There was no I want this and must have that, with a clear mental image of what it was she desired and expected to receive; and that was the most curious thing about it all. She desired no say in the matter. She would abide by her grassy oracle's decision. All she need do was ask and she would be answered: for had she not been answered swiftly and suddenly when she had given up all hope of having been heard?

She was large now and she moved much less quickly. From the start she had taken sparse interest in the preparations which were going on around her and had left to the ecstatic Dora the many duties connected with nursery furnishings and nursery maids, secretly amused at the thought that the newcomer would require none of these things or persons. But she came very near to anger on finding that the sceptre of all this nursery world was to be borne by a certain Sophia Peadbury, a stout rock-like creature of fifty summers and more, with a square of grey unpolished face; very clean, very correct, conspicuously null.

To Dora she protested.

She had thought it understood that there were to be only young light-footed people in the nurseries.

Young people, countered Dora nonplussed, were very well for the lighter duties, but one must have some one really capable and trustworthy when it comes to dealing with a small child. And her references were excellent. She was with the Downham-Renshaws and the Gawtrys, and was especially and carefully recommended.

So she understood that it was a family decision, and nothing whatever to do with her. It was recognised that such decisions never had, and were unalterable.

Attempting flippancy she wondered: why not Stephen's old nurse?

It had been suggested, when it was remembered that she died two years ago. Would she not have been too old? Eighty-nine; though with all her faculties about her. Did you never see her? She lived in that absurd cottage you always point to just beyond Aldbury Cross. Dora would not have her looking so hurt. It was for the best, the child's best.

She made no further protest. She knew it was useless to let it be seen how deeply she felt about it because to Dora her resentment must seem merely personal and directed against the family. But she was hurt, more hurt than she cared to admit for she must allow no secondary thoughts to divert her mind from its singleness of purpose; and she brooded over it this grey and saddening afternoon in early March as she sat on the stone edge of the lily pond goading with her finger a floating leaf until the water rolled over it, took possession of it and tried heavily to drag it down.

She was on her way back to the house from her grassy solitude and whether because being heavy she grew more easily tired or because the thought of returning immediately to the house was distasteful to her, she sat down to rest. An eighteenth-century nymph on her carved moss-grown pedestal leapt up from the centre of the pool in all her shoddy exaggeration and clumsy effectiveness. Because of a somewhat harassed and weary smile, effaced as it were by a green dipped finger in the days when the conch shells clasped so delicately between her fingers had played water on her face with monotonous insistence, Ruth always thought that she looked more like a young lady who had lost her clothes than like one who should be unaware of what clothes might be.

Then she was not to have (not only as she had expected but had never questioned) she was not to have healthy youthful faces to bend over it, and healthy youthful teeth to smile down on it, and crisp, youthful fingers to handle it, and youthful eyes, and quick youthful voices that had not been trained to servility and righteousness. She was to have the heavy, the conformable, the unwisdom of the too-well-bred. For any child she would have resented this dull and steady routine of guidance; this foreshadowing of the inevitable pleasant-nursery product. For the new and strange being which slowly her mind was bringing to perfection in her womb her resentment was deep and critical.

—You will not like it, said Ruth to the edge of flinty stone which could be seen in the distance half hidden by labyrinths of yew hedge, spacious towering single trees, old walls enclosing separate and tidy gardens, littering the ground which separated her from the house. You will not like it, and it will understand you as little as I do.

That she did not belong she had always known. What until recently she had not known was how very much she did not desire to belong. Which was what Stephen's mother could not forgive in her. There was no gratitude in the girl. Amiable-mannered, quiet and quiet-looking enough, though what Stephen could see in the girl who compared unfavourably, most unfavourably as she had said from the first. People liked and accepted her. Yet impossible, and she could not rid herself of the thought—who had had to stand by, unwilling spectator, and watch the whole unfortunate affair and make the best of it and smile the formal smile she had been taught early, used all her life and found sufficient—that the girl did not realise she had been lifted from genteel poverty to position and plenty. She could not accept (who saw mankind divided by divine and unerring right into two unalterable groups, the group which at Christmas and for sickness dispensed blankets and jars of calves'-foot jelly and the group which at Christmas and during sickness received the blankets and jars of calves'-foot jelly) this total absence of humility, of correct understanding, of grateful acknowledgement. The girl had been rescued from genteel poverty by the foolhardiness of her son without so much as a thank you or a timid smile. It was not easy to forgive her that.

She did not know that Ruth was without gratitude because without knowledge of what genteel poverty might be. Her father's fault, of course. His ideas on education were so far ahead of his times that the book he wrote on his method in 1888 (or was that the year of its publication?) when Ruth was six years old and the only other person in the world presumably aware that such a system existed, was not heard of until about 1909 when Professor August Braunschweig of Stuttgart, discovering the work through a cursory reference in a catalogue of educational text books, descended on the surprised publishers who after considerable delay unearthed a copy (the great moment of my life, the old man was known to say in after years) and was practically handed over the translation and foreign rights as a gift; and having shut himself up for the better part of a year exploded on the german educational world the wonders of the Justin Dalby method. Later Professor Braunschweig following up his success with a Life of his hero, arrived in Havre on a long and enthralling visit to M. Jacques La Thangue, Dalby's life-long friend, with whose assistance, notably in the matter of dates and letters and remembered conversational-scraps, Braunschweig compiled that memorable biography which in its english translation *Dalby of Litherton* sent astonished educational authorities hurrying to their library shelves to see whether by any chance, mislaid, one could never tell.

Arrived in the drear inconspicuous Hampshire townlet Braunschweig found that little if anything was remembered of his hero, except that he died of paralysis in 1904 after having been in a mental home for more than a year following a stroke. That the only person who could have given him such information as he desired was Dalby's housekeeper, Emma Grier, who had died aged seventy-four a month after hearing of her master's death. That he was a widower, no one having seen his wife who died in childbed they said; and had come to Litherton when his little girl was two years old and opened his school on the outskirts near

Barton Common. His daughter? well, she had gone away after his death and had not come back since, nor heard of, married some said, though no one knew rightly to whom; some saying she had gone to live abroad leaving no word at all behind her, things get about and people talk; anyway, she had not been heard of, had not come back, and was not likely to now; and besides you never could tell for the Professor himself was queer at times and kept to himself a great deal and had no friends in the neighbourhood.

They could however point to his grave, of which Professor Braunschweig after placing thereon a large and formal laurel wreath threaded with crimson ribbon and getting the sexton to help him neaten the few square feet of forlorn and neglected earth, took several photographs. They could also point to the rambling creeper-covered two-storey house which had been his school and of which the Professor took several more photographs; as also views of the little town and the cliffs and the sea surrounding and containing it.

Before leaving Litherton which he loathed, partly for its crass and childish ignorance of the daily life of his idol, and partly because the good german was surfeited with the drab and ill-cooked food peculiar to english country inns with their insular insistence on bad beer and whisky, both of which he found undrinkable, he had a stroke of unexpected good fortune. He found in a small dilapidated shop in the High Street two photographs of Justin Dalby. That one in profile, maned and serene as Asclepius, which not unnaturally was the cause of that sustained heroic and fate-defying tone adopted as characteristic of the man by his biographer, and which was later to puzzle and disquiet Ruth who found only the quality of heart-ache in her father's gentle and bewildered face. The other a full-length picture in which he held on his knee a staring child whose long loose curls were brushed gravely from her face, held by a wide black velvet ribbon round her little skull, and ending in a bow on the top of her head. Had Professor Braunschweig studied this photograph more carefully there would have been a great deal less of that thunder-defying splendour in the portrait of his hero which he gave to the world. It never occurred to the excellent biographer lost in opalescent clouds of hero-worship, of theories, notebooks, of the fate-shattering neglect of genius, that Justin Dalby had himself put that ribbon round his daughter's little skull, and following her instructions had tied with infinite humour and patience that precise black velvet bow.

At school she had been called My-Father-Says. At the end of her first term she arrived home ill, dispirited, and nervous, and a week before the holidays ended there had been a frightful day of hysteria and shuddering and teeth-chattering incoherence. Finally after much persuasion she had showed him the long mark across her palm which she had kept so carefully hidden and where she had been burnt with a poker for misunderstanding some trifling clause in an uncertain code of honour. More unbearable than the burn which didn't hurt now at all, was that they sneered at her unconscious and perpetual references to her father, at her clothes, at her silence which they interpreted as sullenness, at her shyness which they mistook for sulkiness. In short she had been put through all the subtleties of torture inflicted by boisterous normal school children on the retiring and abnormal child. And it was all as nothing compared with her hourly longing to be with her father again.

During her single term at school there was a girl who was very kind to her, came to her rescue on more than one occasion, took her under her protection for she was older than Ruth, came to stay at Litherton, came even now and then to spend her holidays with Ruth and her father and Mrs Grier in the cottage he took year after year beyond Portloe. It was a curious protective friendship this of the older girl for Ruth, the more so because nothing could have been more simple or unexciting than the quiet Dalby household. Whereas after her father's death when Ruth for the first time in her life was seriously ill and lost masses of her shadowy and beautiful hair, Dora taking charge of her again as if she had been a child, carried her off to her lovely home Wrockram, that show-place of the North, where Ruth was never to forget the summer noons through which in her convalescence, drowsing on cushions on the floor of the boat, she seemed to glide over the lake with its hundred turnings, its dragon-fly murmurings, its pale enchanted willows mirrored in the glazed water; and where the following year she met Stephen.

She was not then altogether to blame for her lack of gratitude at being, what were the words?, lifted from genteel poverty to position and plenty. The distinction her father had made as between races, peoples, classes, differed in many ways from the distinctions common to his day (his book being written, or was it published? in 1888) which was a pleasant one of smug imperialism, good queens and good will; and particularly did they differ in their not being calculated on a monetary or patriotic basis. Long before the days of an H. G. Wells

popular History of the World on every schoolroom bookshelf together
with the mob-educative value of the penny daily newspapers showing
that other strips of land can exist and be inhabited by people not neces-
sarily frogs or fools or ignoramuses or bullies, the obscure schoolmaster
was insisting in his obscure and modest study that it is as unwise as it is
impossible to define where races begin, end, and merge, as it is to
define where art and the noises of races such as music and speech begin,
end, and merge.

How well she remembered her father telling her that a man is his
own reward or his own punishment. Nothing, how well she remembered that dear homily of his!, nothing could alter that. You can no
more reward or punish another human being, Ruth, than that being can
reward or punish you. And forgiveness. That was the most ludicrous
pretence of them all! Never use the word, tear it out, make a little ball
of it and throw it in the fire. There was no such thing.

And that afternoon on which, returning from her first Sunday school
where Mrs Grier had insisted on taking her (for she had her rights said
Emma Grier and one was, after looking after her moonstruck master,
to see that his little girl—his little orphan as she called Ruth—was
given a good christian grounding in the Word) and over the Sunday
crumpets and Emma's Sunday potato-cakes in father's brownly warm
and littered study, she had insisted on piping out all that she had heard,
and had come to the story of the Tribute unto Cæsar and her father had
put down his tea-cup with a great laugh and said: Who but Voltaire
could have countered that so neatly? (For he taught her to love France
and the french whom he called the modern and socratic beacon of the
world.) Ah, that was the way to learn one's lessons! Wrapping up
warmly after tea (Emma saw to that) and striding over the cliffs towards
Barton shouting after father in one's best french Voltaire's *Discourse on
Moderation* in a thin pointed voice, as one struggled against the sea-wind
that gathered the words out of one's mouth and rushed them away
beyond reach unless one held on and got in first.

There was the day on which for the first time he made her walk barefooted on the grass. The indignant Emma at an upper window shouting
that he was killing his own child, a murderer before the Lord, and that
if she came to die, poor creature, she Emma was a witness and would
tell all that she knew. But Ruth survived to repeat the experiment every
morning, putting herself as he explained to her in direct contact with
the earth, with the generative power which bore mountains, poured
streams, moved sap. He told her to think of this as she began slowly

crossing the grass backwards and forwards; and sure enough quite soon the soles of her feet would begin to tingle and impelled she knew not how, with Mercury's wings at her heels, she would begin running, faster, faster, laughing, elated, breathless, glowing. With few exceptions he maintained that most of the ills of the body could be cured by walking barefooted on grass. Moreover this in an age when the human female did not walk for two reasons: tight shoes and propriety. And in this age in which bodily movement in the female was restricted and rendered painful by whalebone and yards of heavy unwieldy cloth, he saw to it that his daughter wore warm lightly woven garments bearing from the shoulders and not the waist. (Alas, how exquisitely droll they found this at school!)

Hers was a lonely and blissful childhood belonging wholly to her father. Once when Emma, who took pride in distributing largesse in the shape of cakes and puddings to a group of old women near her home, had left her alone outside the cottage of old Mrs Caithey, the very ancient lady had patted her curls and mumbled something about a pretty mite and a poor motherless little creature. How incensed Ruth had been! Not waiting for Emma to reappear she had run all the way home like a fury to find her father, and it took all his persuasiveness and tact to dissuade her from dragging him back to the cottage at once and showing him to Emma's cronies. Showing them this perfect being and stopping once for all their silly woman's-chatter about poor and motherless.

Unlike most children who have lost their mothers at birth she had felt little desire to hear her mother spoken of, or explained to her, or described. Her father sufficed. Love and passion beyond her years were in the dreams she wrapped him in. He was in turn all the heroes of her favourite legends. It was all she could do sometimes on seeing him return from the town or from a visit, to keep from rushing out to him and crying: O *why* did you tell Polyphemus your *name*? I've been so *anxious* about you. And did you kill the Minotaur? And rout the Danes? And meet the Great Khan face to face? And defy the Tsar of all the Russias?

As they strode together in the grey winter afternoons over the cliffs toward Barton she would invest him with the magic of Wodan, his beard moving in the sea winds and his old black felt hat over his bartered eye, and she would ask him Why father this and Why father that, knowing that the god of wisdom himself was answering her.

The day on which she came to the story of Pallas-Athene springing from the forehead of Zeus her father, was one of extreme emotional content for her. She recognised it at once, this divine symbol of the unity existing between her father and herself. She read and re-read, heart hammering her ribs, eyes round as croquet balls, a smile on her lips, very happy. Everything then tended towards the deification of this rare father! They too recognised him, these divine beings from whom he sprang! Thus and therefore was she born. And secretly studying her father's high and tolerant brow she found the theory not only feasible, but wise and perfect.

Absurd then to expect gratitude when so much had died with her father and in a trance she had been taken away and in a trance had met and married and exchanged twenty years of adoration and constant and satisfying companionship and used and simple rooms and a flowery untidy garden with its beloved orchard and one stubborn old man who had his own way in the kitchen garden no matter what his cranky maaster said and a stern old woman to look after them both, for this cumbersome imposing mansion, grey, lichened, terraced, beautiful in so many ways, pretentious and uncomfortable in so many more, filled with the come-and-go of servants and strangers meaning little, and set on a stretch of land which after two years upon it she was still ignorant as to where it began or ended. Absurd then to resent such casual acceptance by one who not only had never possessed, but had never been instructed in the decent attitudes of mind connected with possession.

She could not help feeling rather as the very young feel when gazing down in to their bowl of breakfast porridge (sugarless again this morning for some excellent if secret reason) they are told not only to eat it up quickly now, but to remember all the poor and homeless children who have no such porridge to come down to in the morning. Well then give them my porridge. Please give them my porridge. Give them all the porridge they want, but do not ask me to share it with them. Let them strut about proud places without beginning or end and strut through the formal pageantry of dead things and dead people, renewing themselves only in ghostly memories of these ghostly selves, which leaves them smiling politely down the centuries, bewildered as the nymph with her features erased as it were by a green-dipped finger. And give them also the Hungerford nose and the Stanner eye; particularly the Stanner eye. For Stephen's mother, as is known, having been a Stanner had brought the Stanner eye to the Hungerford nose: an impregnable alliance. Had not Ruth with a grave patience (which made his mother sometimes wonder whether, after all, there might not be, if not gratitude, at least awe?) listened so often to the serious apportioning of the Eye of the one side and the Nose of the other to those about to be, to those who were, to those who had been? And looked in those large smoke-grey eyes in their grey corrugated setting and tried hard to believe; and loyally tried also not to wonder whether Stephen's nose were not a shade too long and the nostrils a shade too wide for all the moral and physical distinction claimed for it.

The large and known Gainsborough canvas of Miss Thalia Stanner which hangs in the National Gallery (Room VI) is an excellent record of the Stanner eye. A pleasant and elegant young person Miss Thalia, not unlike a pink satin bolster held negligently together by silvery ribbons, the invitation of whose warm and audacious bosom is suddenly and surprisingly withdrawn by the meagre thread of those smiling lips and, above, the large and wintry Stanner eye mist-grey and exquisitely set; eyes which could tear the heart could they weep and irradiate it could they laugh, and are lost, irrevocably lost, by their seeming unawareness of all but themselves and that at which they gaze. As chance wills it, not far away, just round the corner of the next room in fact, fourth canvas on the left on entering, beside the small Romney study of Lady Hamilton vacant-eyed and mouth too far agape, is the Reynolds portrait of Rear-Admiral Sir Lawrence Addeley Hungerford, demonstrating singularly well the strength and weakness of the Hungerford nose. One smiles on first catching sight of that heavy paunched figure, ill-balanced by a face too large and a wig too small, and at the chubby hand thickly fingering the scroll of parchment which, can one doubt?, he has never so much as glanced at; and one is pondering how such facial glow and meaty splendour were matured and maintained in the days before naval seafaring had attained the comfort of a trans-atlantic luxury liner, when by lifting the eyelid one is made aware of the Hungerford nose, elongated, alive, ant-eaterish, setting at naught the ill-balanced wig and hefty paunch.

The Hungerford nose it will be admitted makes one pause. Even as it disappoints it excites. Here is a nose cast to found dynasties; active for scenting power; nervous for prying around Courts and hand-caressing-hand breathing what it has flaired into the ear of Popes. Too short for wisdom; too long for the wilful following of itself around unlit corners. Lamentably a thing of good and evil in equal parts and therefore valueless. In short, a treacherous wise and catholic nose, reduced by generations of ease and prosperity to being nothing more formidable than the touchstone of a small and tradition-sacred family on a small and tradition-sacred island.

Certainly it was not fair to them. They did not deserve this conspirator in their midst, outwardly quietly believing and quietly respectful; who yet recoiled from the humorous possibility of reproducing a Stanner eye as from reproducing a blind eye, and would as soon perpetuate Ganesha's swaying funnel as perpetuate the anachronistic Hungerford nozzle. You will not like it, said Ruth to the edge of flinty stone which could be seen in the distance half-hidden by labyrinths of yew-hedge, spacious towering single trees, old walls enclosing separate and tidy gardens, littering the ground which separated her from the house. You will not like it, and it will understand you as little as I do.

S he smiled at the thought of what they would think of it.

After all, the world did not take so lightly to change now that centuries of religious thought and habit had accustomed it to the belief that man as he existed was the highest form of life god could create. She smiled, thinking of what Minos must have said on being presented with the infant Minotauros for which his wife had pursued her wild and milk-white bull across the woods and hills of Crete. At the river god and the muse with their litter of strange siren daughters, half-woman half-bird, half-woman half-fish. At the dolphined Tritons driving their golden chariots over the floor of the ocean, playing in the sunshine on the white surface of the seas. Was it not a proud day indeed when first the sounding of their conch-shells rocked the waters? And that nameless nymph who gave Hylas to Zeus and to Hermes (for this is a case of disputed paternity), did she not marvel at her first sight of those downy legs and upcurved eye and rejoice as later she was to rejoice and marvel at the shaggy haunches and tufted chin and listen for the sound of his shepherd's pipe of seven reeds and live to know the hills and groves and flowering oaks made sacred to him for ever. And Hera, that malignant and much-tried sister spouse of Zeus. What were her thoughts when the infant centaur burst from that cloud-image fashioned to deceive the lovelorn Ixion? (Was ever excuse of prim and faithless wife so transparent! Yet for Ixion's sake just as well, who knows, for surely a most formidable Royal Personage to love in the flesh.) Did Hera smile, grim sentinel of heaven, the day on which she gave the first centaur to the world and saw its still-soft opaque hoofs seek to adjust themselves to the earth? And in the rare intervals of her slayings and cruelties and jealous womanly treacheries and in her long days bereft of love, pause to wonder at this new and unexpected being she had created? Did it evoke in her a sudden tenderness to watch him leaping and frisking on the grassy slopes of his mountain home, as he learned to plant his milky hoofs more firmly on the stubble of the mountain paths and stampede the herds in his mother's fields and race with them?

Did they play with their children? Who knows? Helplessness was not a virtue to the greeks. Immaturity not a condition that appealed to them.

What a sombre morose day. A grey day, cloud succeeding cloud in a grey sky under which even the new buds looked chilled and the grass seemed to find no warmth in the earth it clung to. Only the nymph smiled her green erased smile. Ruth remembered her father regretting the exploits of Herakles as having caused so much bad art among Hellenic sculptors. What of the naked young men in Arcady's sylvan streams and the post-Canova stone manipulators?

She was still tired and restless as she rose and made her way slowly to the house. Her head ached stubbornly. She wondered how she could avoid Dora, who would notice it at once.

Curious this solicitude in women, these tentacles of tenderness with which they seek to bind those near and dear to them. Was it a defensive weapon this inexhaustible fount of woman's sympathy, this tender interference, this insidious and perpetual warfare of subduing and conquering by dependence on their indispensability; and of making the strong relinquish to it their freedom and their will: as the pathos and helplessness of an infant is set as a trap for those on whom it depends for the continuance and necessities of its life? Was this then the secret dissatisfaction between man and woman this perpetual binding of the strong by the weak, the perpetual triumph of the binder over the bound, the easy unscrupulousness of the weak and the angry helplessness of the strong. Or was it that only woman understood woman: as only man understood man. And but rarely, as with father and myself, man and woman understand one another, and create the perfect human relationship?

Whatever it might be, useless to hope that her headache would escape her friend's vigilant eye and vigilant ministrations. And she was right; Dora came across to her a solicitous frown between her eyes. Where had she been all the afternoon, she had been so anxious; she looked pale, she looked cold, had she not a headache? she looked tired; did she not know that she must not strain herself especially these last weeks. All of which correct and simple statements were countered with a smile and a few correct and reassuring sentences; wishing she could respond more genuinely; wishing she did not resent this evident and unselfish desire to be of use and serve; wishing one did not envy for women that male matter-of-factness of summing up and dismissing that made for hardiness of mind as rough oats made for hardiness of bone.

She was displeased with herself for she was thoroughly ashamed of such rebellious critical moods. It was wrong that she should watch unmoved but for an external politeness, a smile correctly adjusted, a word correctly placed, these ministrations for one's comfort. It was in moments such as that that she would come again to the desire to fathom whatever bound Dora to her with such an urge, such an intensity; almost with the implacability of enmity. A certain wilful helplessness in her appearance, an answering to Dora's need to protect and dominate; who insisted on the very animals about her being docile and grateful: which may account for her dislike of cats, thought Ruth, who adored them. Stephen too was bound to her through this protective need, evoking gratitude, projecting on a lesser and unhappier being the full splendour of one's goodness. She had been sick and heavy with her sorrow and loss when first they met; and what man can resist unhappiness in a woman? Be sad that I may be gay. The giving which is more than the receiving. How otherwise had Stephen gone against his own and his mother's prejudices, and accepted the weariness of her perpetual disapproval and disappointment?

What warm safety in the sound of tea-things moved and the stir of voices (she remembered that she had left her book beside the pond) and fireglow leaping in silver and walnut and touching to reality dark tapestry foliage and umber smiles in faded portraits and Dora's generous and finely drawn head bent over it all, smiling.

And in that gesture, in that familiar half-smile of abnegation and triumph which hovers about women's lips, menacing, indelible, Ruth was aware of the world as the victim of woman's ineradicable possessiveness; that emotional maternal substance which women ooze as a form of adhesive plaster by which mankind is held together, and is decaying.

T he nurse, that mixture of servility and condescension, had arrived. She began at once on her triumphs.

Nurse Gunn. (Putting aside her book, taking the plate on her lap and detaching a grape, Ruth smiled down the years at Nurse Gunn.) An ominous-sounding name but not inappropriate. Direct, ruthless, single-purposed, with a certain metallic imagery suggesting power and action. Death one was assured had here a worthy opponent. One felt he would remember her. One understood he could not ignore her. Above, behind, beneath, about, each bed that Nurse Gunn succoured lurked the Dread Form behaving not unlike Sir Henry Irving in his more tempestuous moments. A simple tenet and an effective one seeing that it put Nurse Gunn on the defensive, and Nurse Gunn on the defensive moved with the wrath of the Lord in her step and the lightning of the righteous in her hand. Helmeted, collared, a vast shining iridescent and bulging breastplate buckled to a twenty-two-inch waistband, and shaking her thermometer as Blake's angels shook their spears; and more effectively.

When Nurse Gunn fought she won. When Nurse Gunn did not win it was because she had been called in too late. Her prowess in snatching corpses from under Death's hollow nose must have been trying in the extreme to that hitherto omniscient gentleman, if only that her manner so lacked respect, so wanted dignity. His swift and icy step was not, it seemed, to Nurse Gunn what it was to the rest of mankind: an utter darkness, an end to all, a dread which words cannot compass and thought dare not. Here was no silent prayer, no secret apprehension, no momentary doubt. Nothing of the frail acolyte and wrestling devil. No wan saint and high-breasted fleshly lady. No mercy-begging Magdalen curtained within her own hair. But a cool tra-la-la and away, a hide-and-seek-and-saw-you-first, a dash of something cool on the near-corpse's damp brow, a now-just-one-leetle-sip-more, a burning tea-spoon pressed to a reviving lip, a that's-right, that's-better on a gay soprano note. And Death was being handed his hat in the hall. Leaving the house with the efficient smiling doctor. Good day, Sir. Good day.

Foiled! Foiled again. And by that bouncing merry little woman with the large simplified face of a crab and the incredibly small mouth which when opened seemed full of rice, overflowing and retained with difficulty.

Those privileged to listen to the chivalric, frequent, withal-modest accounts of these combats became positively afraid of dying on Nurse Gunn's hands, so sure were they that Death on ultimately taking possession must make one pay dearly for such victories. Could such matters be smiled away? One could begin with a tactful but not obse-quious: how delightful to meet you at last. Of course I never quite believed those naïve, those quite too amusing. . . . One could not

expect Nurse Gunn to come to the rescue by playing Sydney Smith to
the worsted and aggrieved schoolmaster who must be off: I pray,
Doctor, do not endorse my sins on their backs. Was she not too busy
endorsing her triumphs almost as ruthlessly?

In fairness to Nurse Gunn it must be told that in her presence her
patients thought but rarely of Death. There was about her a resolution
which made them understand that even should the unexpected happen
and one departed and arrived, Saint Peter would extend an apologetic
hand and say: Ah no, dear lady. Not just yet. There has been a mistake.
Nurse Gunn wants you back.

Mischievous as children they played Nurse Gunn as a game. The
choice was embarrassing. One could have Nurse Gunn and Lady
Titherley Paulton. Or Nurse Gunn and Dr Bonnington Hargreaves.
Or Nurse Gunn and the mother of Lady Alberta Dimming whose
maternal ardour encroached on certain professional duties until an
exasperated Nurse Gunn stood confronting Sir Jasper Rivington:
Unless I am left in complete control of my patient, Sir Jasper, I cannot.
She seemed always to have been bearing down on eminent obstetrical
surgeons and issuing ultimata. There still remained after all these years
that favourite portrait of herself pale, authoritative, white-lipped,
amazonian, moving firmly yet noiselessly over the heavy carpet
towards Sir Angus McHugh (The Royal Accoucheur, emphasised
Nurse Gunn) most reputed obstetrician in two centuries. Sir Angus you
must operate. At once. My duty. Mrs Sibthorpe Hepplethwaite (the
Norfolk Hepplethwaites) lived. But for you, she said. She knew that I
had, well, not ordered, but, well, insisted. Lived, rare bloom in the
herbaceous border of important cases flowering perennially down the
fringes of Nurse Gunn's career and in her patients' memories.

She had been filled with a comic dismay. What malignant or
humorous fate could have dropped this solid talkative mass of all
that she did not want to encounter or be reminded of into the midst of
her exacting and arbitrary urge on the threshold of its fulfilment? She
had found herself, a child again, wheedling her new tyrant into al-
lowing her to leave the house; had had to cajole for permission to
walk five minutes alone in the grounds.

—Who will rid me of this turbulent priestess, she had cried in mock
alarm, running into her in every doorway. Useless. Nurse Gunn inspired

a degree of awe and obedience that a chief inquisitor might well have envied. Many a time she could almost have cried with vexation at seeing these last days of such intense and urgent purport intruded on; their peace, so necessary to her just now, broken in upon and shattered. For a moment it even occurred to her that these meetings were deliberate; that she was being watched. That the inescapableness of Nurse Gunn was a plot. She dismissed this as absurd and as a sign of morbid pre-occupation: although inevitably she had been right. It never occurred to her that she was every bit as unreal to Nurse Gunn as Nurse Gunn was to her. Or that Nurse Gunn after a conversation with Dr Mason had been more than confirmed in her early impression. Such a singular young woman, who seemed to have no idea at all of what was happening to her and had asked none of the usual questions. Asked no questions at all in fact, and stared in comically frightened and surprised manner if the subject was broached. Queer, said Nurse Gunn. And deep.

While Nurse Gunn was being shocked by this discovery, Ruth made one of her own. That not only had Nurse Gunn's patients all been brave and noble but that all the children she had helped into the world had been dear and beautiful. It would seem she could not bring herself to form the word child without the qualifying dear and beautiful. Such a beautiful child. Such a beautiful boy and such a dear little girl. Boys were always beautiful; girls always dear and little.

Decidedly God might have found a nicer way. Why had He been so masculine in His disregard for the acute sensitiveness that He might surely have understood, had He given it thought, a woman feels at the culmination, at the anticlimax? One understood that fresh from creating mountains and releasing torrents; but He might at least have made it a private matter; quick, secret, and alone. It was inexcusable. It was obvious that He had had no woman to advise Him on the subject. He was directly responsible for the presence of Nurse Gunn! Knowing how absurd she was being, Ruth still could not help feeling it as the supreme humiliation and absurdity that one must deliver oneself into the hands of total strangers at the most weird and aweful moment of one's life: and it hurt her as something physical that others should first see and handle the new and strange being which she had brought to perfection in her body.

And all at once it seemed equally wrong to her to bear her child in a bed. Especially in this heavy portentous canopied tomb of a bed with its sly and hearty boast of the loves and births and deaths which had filled its capacious and elaborate lap for the last three hundred years. Used.

Worn out. Old. Stale with stale memories of repeated and familiar sights. How had it happened that every thing vital had been reduced to the limits of four walls, bringing shame and fear with them? One should be born on hills, on clouds, near streams, in woods, on open and pleasant spaces. Civilisation. Fear of unsheltered spaces. Too many walls inside which things were performed in fear and shame.

She grew so easily tired and restless indoors. They would not let her go to her woods now, nor beyond a stone's-throw of the house. (Then Stephen shall throw a stone for me Ruth had insisted slyly, losing patience; leading him to the window and pointing in the direction in which she wanted to go, and Stephen to her amazement and delight had thrown a stone which no one saw fall. Even then, for all the fun and chaffing it had caused, they would not let her go after it.) They feared for her. Ever since he had died she seemed to have been surrounded by people who feared for her; and yet she had no fear for herself or the new thing her mind had perfected, and which her body would soon reject.

The Apollo-image, that at least had been a wise direction of consciousness; yet, there again, Apollo, with Socrates on the potter's ware at their very door! Still, there was something adequately wise and noble in such an impersonal choice as beauty: which was more than could be said for the monstrous fetish of the Family which women had since created for themselves. Shoemaker no higher than the shoe. Woman no further than your immediate environment. To fail to create an Apollo was at worst a dignified defeat: to succeed in getting a family likeness at best a doubtful triumph. Look! his father's nose. The blue of his mother's eye. Do you not think that this is a perfect imitation of myself, of us, of my great-grandfather, of his mother's mother's mother, of everything that has been in the Family since its inception?

The monstrous conceit that birth was limited to the reproduction of imperfections hallowed by their association with oneself! Where was man's humility, his sense of the ridiculous? Bred his beasts in fear and reverence; himself as an after-thought; clipped ears and docked tails; paid stud fees that would keep a regiment in food and drink for half a year; who could not see a petal too long red without worrying it to purple. Was this then why man had ceased to evolve: as though a doubtful perfection had been attained? And having ceased to evolve had fallen back on invention: a crutch for an able leg?

Was it not exasperating the ineffectiveness of man? Take for instance all this talk raging around flying. Were they not beside themselves just now, incredulous, eager, partisans, sceptics? Would it one day be possible to remain in the air for two entire hours? Or fly above long stretches of water? A joke in poor taste. A madman's hallucination. Actually man was to attempt to float on the air in a box of a machine with wings to bear it up? A box with wings! And they were proud of it or angry at it and one and all fearful of it.

Why, man had dreamt of wings since the moment he first, with shaded eyes, stared at something swift and purposeful flashing high above his head through space, and grown sad (for there is no sight more melancholy than that of birds winging across skies, grave arrows from some celestial bow) at the knowledge of his two stationary feet: on earth, in earth, of earth; his heart and eyes taking the flight his feet could not follow. Who knew in what first dawn this urge came to man? (He would have known. He would have told me, thought Ruth.) The earliest Art had traces of it; stiff broad feathery boards rising from shoulder blades; some winged their beasts; others their gods; others their victories; all, their supermen.

Always this thought of wings lifting man to godhead. Knowing their lack, sensing their insufficiency, content to imagine their desires instead of creating them! Their little box with wings attached was nothing: was less than nothing, poor travesty of man's first awe! Women could have shown them that. Women could have shown them how wings are made had they taken heed and used wisely the centuries of thought and prayer. What Leonardo had dared dream woman could have dared achieve. Piglierà il volo il grande uccello . . . empiendo l'universo di stupore, empiendo di sua fama tutte le scritture e gloria eterna al loco dove nacque. . . . Hers the nest in which to hatch that dream and people those skies. Vagliami il lungo studio e il grande amore! Those were words to emboss in brave lettering on the banner of one's soul! Swiftness of leg should have bred hoofs; swiftness of thought wings; swiftness of mechanical labour a Siva-like many-handedness. Only thus in its never-ending combinations should man have achieved that which he desired and envied; have evolved instead of atrophied, and been born new instead of old; new, strange, and different. (So that there would always have been such fun in it, as she put it to herself.)

Without this knowledge of something new and rare to sustain her she would still have been as unreconciled and appalled as in the first bitter weeks of her pregnancy. She spent the last few days in an exaltation bordering at moments on frenzy. Enclosed within herself as she had been since her father's death, her sense of his loss was most acute now that all that she had since become cried out to him to be near her now when most she needed him. That apart she was emptied of all emotion save a sense of boundless serenity and power. She had no misgivings and no fears. She felt abundantly strong and eager. She thought of the dreams and legends of her youth and knew that no child conceived and sired as she had been could give birth to a thing commonplace or usual. As she had made no specific demands, had projected no definite mind-image, she could not anticipate. Nor did she desire to. How often later she was to reiterate this in moments of half-hearted self-justification and derive some measure of comfort from it!

She bore her child on the evening of June 5, 1907, after several hours of prolonged pain in which she had the curious and appalling impression of being burned alive. As she sank in a heavy stupor of relief and tiredness she seemed to catch the echo of a distant voice murmuring: such a beautiful boy. But that might have been a dream. She laughed weakly.

Instead of a cool and normal awakening she woke with fever and grew worse as the morning wore on. For almost a month she was ill; often delirious; rarely altogether conscious of what was happening about her or what had become of her. But by the first week in July she was being propped up on her pillows aware of a wealth of pale summer flowers about her, as soft movements from the open windows bore their presence to her in sudden waves of flower-incense.

Everyone about her was very quiet and gentle. She would have thought them almost sad had she been able to gather her thoughts together with any sureness. But she was tired. She had had a child; that was why she had been ill. From a dense bundle of ribbon and lace, which became so heavy when placed in her arms that, startled, she could not hold it, peered a nebulous round face, a sparse fluff covering its minute veined skull. Two grey eyes widely spaced and set stared at her and stared. Two fists of a surprising minute perfection, clenched themselves. They told her it was a boy and, still startled, she was astonished and delighted at its winsome and minute perfection.

—Is he not beautiful? hazarded Ruth. Everyone agreed with her, gently and kindly. She was growing strong again. Something troubled and escaped her, as with children who turn suddenly, warily, and leap in the very centre of their shadow only to find it once more ahead of them, intangible, tormenting.

Late one afternoon, half-waking from a short troubled sleep, she heard a woman's voice saying mournfully, distinctly: but later Nurse he may walk? and a woman's voice deferential but decided: O no. There is no question of that. You can see for yourself that that . . .

She must have made some movement or sound for the voices ceased and some-one stood beside her bed. She asked to see her child. When it was brought and she had asked them to undress it, unwrap it, and they hesitated saying something vague about the chill and not yet being too strong, she began with calm and steady fingers untying the innumerable ribbons that held him together. The child made no sound. He seemed in no way to resent his stripping; seemed indeed hardly aware of it. Hastily windows were being shut and gentle remonstrances continued, as though sudden noise could in some way relieve the tension.

He was beautifully whole and finished; except for his feet. They hung loose and shapeless from the ankle, soft loose pads of waxen flesh. She stared at them unable to bring herself to take them in her hand or touch them. She knew without knowing how she knew that such a newly created being gathers itself together in its feet, grasps with them, beats at the air with them, eagerly draws them in in small soft folds, and with all the hunger of its new-found energy shoots them out again, bending them, curving them, waving them to the rhythm of its new-struggling animal restlessness. She knew that this restlessness continually washing over him in a wave should be gathering him in an ebb and flow of folds and wrinkles. Knowing this she raised her eyes from the loose formless pads of waxen flesh that were his feet to his impassive infant face in which two light eyes widely spaced and set stared at her and stared; and this time she understood the vacant fixity of his infant stare and his utter soundlessness and immobility.

She was sobered and appalled. It was terrible to her. It was as though in a drunken stupor one man had hit another, and they came and said to him: he is dead.

At the foot of the hillock round which Graziella had vanished something heavy and black was moving among the vines. Padre Antonio punctual to the minute was returning from the seminary at Foria Ponte. And at exactly this moment of each afternoon (was it for this she sat there?) she would hear again the crash of Uller's fist on the stone edge of the balcony, see a palette knife describing circles in the direction of the approaching priest, catch the echo of a voice thundering in ill-natured contempt: here comes God's beetle.

A dull beating of muffled drums, a grinding wail not unlike that of a rabbit snared, the gathering murmur of threats: the distant thunder heralding the coming storm of hoofs and blows that would crash past the house now that the men had started for home and those making for Sant' Anna branched off the main road and took the steep path past the house leading to the hills. Here began the ascent and here the place to make the beasts understand that there was work to be done, and a good stick was of the company to ensure its doing.

At first for a very long time on hearing the warning rumble Ruth would fly to the back of the house, to the long stone kitchen where Lisetta at this hour was busy over her charcoal fire, to hide herself and be out of hearing when the storm broke. She could not bear the shrill curses and crackling whips and heavy buttock-blows as the beasts tore by, panic in their hoofs.

—How can they be so cruel! She would stammer to Lisetta, holding her hands over her eyes, aghast at the pleasure it would have given her to rush out in the road, wrest the sticks from the men and bring them down on their own backs, thrashing them down on to the ground, striking them heavily about the eyes and face as in their slyer moments they struck their beasts.

—Macchè, macchè, who is cruel? Do you not see how hard they work themselves? Five times as hard as they can ever get their beasts to work. Pity the men, said Lisetta dismissing it impatiently; it is sadder to be the tamer than the lion.

In time she came also to see it in its truer light and to justify the blows by the prodigious display of sustained energy the men put up daily, year in year out. But even now at times she could still feel the blows on her own back, and could still dread their muted approach as acutely as on hearing it for the first time. The logic of the thing she understood. Crude nature against crude nature was their affair, with a turn of the quick head and a spit true-aimed over the shoulder. It was not easy to regard one's beast in heroic light with one's own feet thick with blisters, and one's own back aching under a load almost as heavy and a march every bit as long. Then why should the sight of a man sweating under a load too large for him arouse in her less pity than the sight of a beast overladen and the sound of blows and galloping hoofs?

Why should the cry of the little goat tied with the ridiculously thick rope to the wall of the house in the hollow which she overlooked, weigh on her heart with a sense of injustice and cruelty? He began crying as the sun went down and continued well into the night: such reproach in his tremulous bleat. Earlier in the week she had noticed him tossing his legs about sideways in a young drunken leggy run; out of tune, out of time. They had hung his food, some strings of vine and laurel leaves around his neck; and there he tossed, fresh from some Pompeian fresco, very lost, very appealing. Some-one was sick in the house: the extra cup of milk was needed. Hitched to the wall with his mother answering him at intervals from the other side of it, he threw out his sad little stutter of self-pity. He would complain: he insisted on complaining. Now and again there came the banging of a door and an angry sound and then a scurry of hoofs. A short pause and away he went echoing through the night silence. One could not walk into another's house and say: here is the fraction of a penny with which to buy that extra cup of milk of which he robs his mother. And Ruth who also could be lost in something near to panic when night fell, would lean alert in her chair or lie awake on her bed reading in his silly young shivery bleats so very much more than there was to them.

Yet the sound of Giovina crying, the never-ending irritable drone of a tired child, awoke in her only acute vexation and dislike.

She could no more explain her attitude than understand theirs. Why they picked up and swung kittens by their hind legs. Or put large birds in small cages. Or how it had been possible for Graziella, herself large and proud with child, to shoot out a foot slyly under the table and jab at the heavy belly of the thin grey cat prowling around warily for scraps.

The last evening was like the first. The afternoon would break imperceptibly between the sly-faced gentle goats swinging down the saracen road. The women and children moving well-wards. The officious shriek of the passenger boat. The bells of San Soccorso (wherein hung the sinister black Christ in his barbaric crimson robe and golden turban, soiled now but horrible, a real idol. The saraceni threw it in the sea and when it came out it was that colour. But the turban? The eastern robe? That all came out of the water too. But how? Ah, well, the saints alone could answer that.) rocking the air with shrill and monotonous clamour. On the edge of the Bay the gathering clouds preparing for an Ascension. God's beetle appearing among the vines, stopping a moment in full view of the balcony to mop his head with a large blue handkerchief and look up, deliberately surprising himself at the sight of her,

and passing the time of day. The thud of hoofs flying past the house and
dwindling to their first vagueness and out of hearing. The bats rushing
past at which the children threw pieces of light-coloured rag loaded
with stones or earth to bring them low, scattering as they swooped. A
settling back into the evening quiet in a muted orchestration of scent
and sound. The pale long ethereal strips of maize glowing in the
gradual dusk like tall headless lilies. The dark pinewoods blurred to the
consistency of wet moss. The darkening hilly background of the coast,
crisp, one-dimensional. Strings of light appearing on the horizon,
drawing nearer at intervals as the island lit up. Little Maria creeping on
the veranda and squatting on her haunches in a corner, her pale candle-
grease face translucent in the shadow. The sound of sudden increased
activity below and a voice crying: *Signor'* v-i-e-n-, vien'mangiar'.

Down the stone steps of the balcony she would go, the day's papers
or a book under an arm, through to the back of the house, across the
long stone kitchen, out on to the vine-thatched *terrazza* where Lisetta's
modest *ristorante al mare* looked out from its rocky eminence over the
narrow strip of sandy beach and the long stretch of water; the misty
outer edges of which now showed pin-pricks of light near Gaeta.

Since her first sight of it Ruth had loved this terrace on the sea and
had chosen her place at the far edge of it, opposite the narrow path cut
in the rock by which the children, the fishermen, and anyone belonging to the house, climbed up from the beach. At night it was all a grave
smoky blue in which the terrace, the sands, the sea, left the sky only
where the stars began. On her table a lamp burned. Lisetta was always
urging on her more light, was always repeating that the electric light
from the house would be extended to the terrace. But she would have
none of it. She loved her lamp. Any suggestion or attempt to alter or
displace things as she knew them always upset her. She liked what she
called her blindman's ways; her ability to find anything with her eyes
shut.

At night at the centre-table the men played cards. A candle lighting
one side of their sun-dried faces in strong Ribera effect cast heavy
shadows down their long spanish noses; gouging out their eyes, hol-
lowing their lean cheeks, throwing into relief their fine white teeth as
they moved their mouths now and then in a half-laugh and a short jerk
of the head. At their elbows the tumblers of heady scented Forian wine
(which the outside world knows ill and overmuch-handled as Lacrimæ
Christi) caught the candle's eye and shone like dull topaz lamps about
the rough wine-spilled table. They rarely laughed outright or made

much noise: as though in emerging from their shadow-selves they must dissolve on the common air. After the perfunctory evening greeting to the eccentric englishwoman they ignored her; unless a newcomer with them had just heard her story and must take long under-eyelid looks at her until, his curiosity sated, he could ignore her with the rest.

A sight of which she never tired. Every night would find them in the same positions, in the same light, at the same game. Whether the faces of the players were the same was of no importance: there could be only young or old versions of the one theme. A few drinking-boys' heads, a few Spagnoletto saints regretting their desert-fasts emaciation, sat together at an inn table and discovered that wine was good and that they were by no means as saintly as they had supposed; which made them jerk their heads at intervals and bare their teeth. Such was her idea of art: a pretty trick of ready-made shadow and a ready-made masterpiece ready to the artist's brush. It pleased her. (She had tried to make Uller paint them and had been surprised and silenced by the vehemence with which he had cursed the whole damned School, shouting loudly for electric light: the salvation of Art. Of the world seeing that it let the sun shine all night, and only by light could one paint. For paint is colour: not excrement. And now its torch had been handed to night. Aired, exposed the darkness and rubbish accumulated through centuries of candlelight. Ordered Lisetta to inform him immediately why she pandered to the fifth-rate taste of genteel englishwomen and continued upholding the barbarous and insanitary customs of her ancestors. Told her to tie strings of tri-colour lights along the vines and walls as all patriotic italian inn-keepers should. And the music? Where was the gramophone? None of your tremoloing brigands. If he wanted to return to Sorrento, shouted Uller flushed with the sound of himself and as usual at his most loud and effective when he had succeeded in making her face retire within itself as it were, drop down its curtains, dissociate itself completely before the handful of italians from his street-boy rudenesses, if he wanted to return to Sorrento he'd make up his own mind about it and not be driven there to escape demented guitarists trying their moonlight-and-napoli aphrodisiac on sluggish tourists. Rows of red white and green lights glaring down in hard icy stare on the tables and a gramophone blaring any popular tune of the moment: and let the whole island in to caper to it and drive the *tenebrosi* and their sham picturesque that quickened the heartbeats of english spinsters back to the darkness of the Michelangelos (the curse of art, that man!) let loose over europe, and from which, thank God, they were slowly but at last emerging.)

Small green lizards, elegant miniature crocodiles, darted after flies on the evening walls. From where she sat she could see the full uddery bladders gleaming through the darkness of the kitchen, strung among the strings of garlic and sausage hanging from the heavy whitewashed beams, richly golden as old amber or polished ivory of great age.

I n such manner from first to last night fell for her. Each incident tallied: except that the Concettas or Giovannis or Graziellas or any other of the innumerable children about the place, grew and made way for the Giovannas the Peppes the Marias to bring the offering of their small candle-grease faces to glow in the shadow; except that Uller had come, had gone; except that the sun had not exhausted its many gracious or angry ways of retiring; nor the moon of appearing; nor the clouds of transforming themselves into the likeliest pattern to harmonise with these beginnings and endings, these departures and arrivals.

Remained the evening meal to be eaten, after which Lisetta, bringing herself the coffee to the table, would fetch her sewing or embroidery or a small heap of those very clean very coarse table-napkins she had all but respun with her darning, and rest herself for an hour or so: an indispensable item of the evening ritual. The two women talked together in low friendly voices. Ruth read aloud extracts from the day's papers. Again Lisetta was surprised at everything. Still surprised at everything. Especially did she like to hear about the road accidents. Again they appalled and delighted her. Still appalled and delighted her, although now they were so frequent and so similar with their same number of motor-cars running into the same number of pedestrians and the same number of pedestrians running under the same number of motor-cars, that that alone should have cooled Lisetta's ardour and pleasure. On the contrary they grew on what they fed: so that by now only a really ruthless train-smash could distract her attention from man and machine in conflict: and what followed for the man. And Ruth read on and on, prolonging the agony for Lisetta and for herself. A treat for Lisetta; a respite for herself.

For after that the evening was at an end and she must go up to the room where Richard slept. Came the scene for which the whole evening had set itself. She had been waiting for this. As something she dared not finger or look at it had lain on the floor of her mind while the sky went through its nightly performance, the children and passers-by ranged themselves in their order, the orchestration of sound and colour swelled and diminished, the men played cards during the interval, she herself going through her leading part among them all, taking her cue with easy familiarity about the shadow stage with its shadow background. And it was not only the evening that passed in preparation for it. That was an untrue and ineffectual evasion. In a sense the whole day was a preparation. The whole night. Waking and sleeping was a preparation. Eating, reading, watching was a preparation. The thing was inescapable. No sooner did she leave him than she was preparing herself to see him again.

Not that she did not see him in the daytime. She did, seeing that he was bound to be around the corner if one turned it. But that mattered little. In the daytime he meant little to her. He was but one of the many players among whom she also moved. In the daytime she could endure him because in the light he did not reproach her. In the light he was not hers. He did not belong especially to her. He might belong to anyone; to whoever was with him and attending him at the moment. Not more to her than to anyone else. All took their share in him. In the daylight he had no claim on her. Or comparatively small claim. For in the day she was distracted and impersonal. The daylight saved her. The daylight always saved her. And that was why when it began to fail, when it began gradually to give way to darkness she became precise in her movements, as though she would fall, knowing them as a sleepwalker knows doors and stairs and passes them with safety and sureness. Until the moment came for her to leave the table and find herself in his room, awake.

She thought it was only as night fell that such preparation had been shaping itself at the back of her mind. She had feared and put it from her all the day. But she did not know this. Only at night it was no longer possible to ignore it and so she was afraid of the night. When night fell she died utterly. She was afraid. She was wretched. Lately she had come to fear the night as an unhappy man fears sleep for the recurring nightmare that must come with it. At times she could have howled with fear like a child waking from an ugly dream and aware that reality may be but the continuance of it. Because her soul was sick: and only robust souls can treat night with indifference and connect it with the rotations of the earth, and pretend that it is no stranger than the day.

Each night she went to her son's room to wish him good-night and see that he was comfortable, and bend over him as a woman bends over her child and watches its sleeping face. Or rather seeing that it was

manifestly absurd for her to wish him good-night or for her to take
delight in his quiescent face, she went each night to her son's room
mentally wringing her Macbethan hands which not all the perfumes of
arabia etc. But Lady Macbeth, it had once occurred to her in one of
those moments when she could stir up a certain grim laughter at the
folly of her self-imposed and never-ending penance, at the useless
martyrdom which she had taken upon herself in a moment of fervour
and repentance, Lady Macbeth did not have to live with the corpse.
Decidedly Lady Macbeth did not have to live with the corpse. And she
would writhe with dry laughter at the thought of the Macbeths with an
unshakeoffable Banquo planted at their table, obstinately standing his
ghostly ground and stubbornly fixing them with his blood-caked eye
over their porringers.

They would have grown used to it. Custom stales. Custom would
have dulled the fire in Banquo's eye and the remorse in his hosts'
hearts. A few more years and they would scarcely have looked over the
edge of their bowls to see if it were fixing them. And had it been they'd
have yawned in it, the grotesque unwinking carnival eye with red-stuff
on it!

Not so with Ruth who had had no legend to bring her to life or
relieve her of it and of her corpse and its responsibility. So that she had
had to learn her lesson: that tomorrow always comes. Only in youth
can one believe that one will die in the night. That mercifully no day
will seek one out. That one will sleep for ever in one's pain, nursed on
the sleep-sea on which, for the eternity of a few kind hours, one sinks.
But tomorrow always comes. The day returns. Too soon: but returns.
And when at last one accepts this adolescence has been left behind:
though one is seventy.

S he had not always felt this about going up to see him and say good-
night. In the beginning it had been a comparatively easy, almost a
natural, task. Even when Uller was there her attitude had not changed.
She had always been somewhat afraid of the darkness which falls with
such remorseless certainty. Only recently had it become a menace. Only
recently had she become aware of how very much she dreaded her
nocturnal visits to her son. Possibly the dread had always been there in a
half-hearted way, but now it was as though being tired of her long vigil
with herself she had transferred it to a horror of the thing responsible

for it. Which was absurd, for she alone was responsible for it. She had lived a long time with her own guilt. Possibly she was tiring of it. Possibly she was thinking that perhaps she had paid. Not in full, but in great part: anyway, enough. Lately she had taken to insisting to herself that as he did not know her when she came, or know that she came; and that therefore as he did not know her. . . . She had fallen as far from grace as that! Coward, coward, she said. And she knew it and despised herself and was restless. Lately she had grown restless. But she went upstairs at night just the same.

That measure of calm and quiescence which so many years had built up was gone. Gone suddenly: but why? Outwardly nothing had altered. Each day for twenty-two years had been much the same, passing out down the road with the smooth gentle-faced goats. She herself noticed no change. Certainly no regrets. Put back the clock twenty-two years and she would have done the same thing again. She would have accepted the monstrous thing that she had done and taken the consequences. Certainly she had no regrets. She was being suddenly confronted with something much more difficult to handle: doubts.

During his childhood's years it had all been so much more difficult for her to realise. Or rather so much more easy to ignore. And of course the glamour of the thing was still on her. Through all the horror at what she had done the glamour was there. Was (who knows?) still there. Put back the clock twenty-three years and she would still do very much the same thing. She would still try. She still thought much about mankind as she had thought then. Even though with years her ideas had altered about many things and she knew that she had been wrong and foolishly young and romantic and trustful. Though she knew that there is but one purpose in life. Man woman and child and child and child. Woman and child. Wash child, wash corpse. That was all there was to it. That was all there should be to it. Could be to it. Woman from the neck downward. Man from the neck downward and upward, as he chose. But for woman no choice. I think, Stephen. I think. I think I carry my womb in my forehead. And she did. And still did. And always would. Because some there are whose souls are more pregnant than their bodies. No, Socrates. And no one has ever thought of applying that to women, because women, Dora. From the neck down, breasts and thighs and pelvic bone. And for head an enlarged heart. A fatty noble heart swollen with appropriate emotions.

Faced with his useless feet and staring silence she had known at once that she was wrong. And even had she not known it, that was soon learned in this land of old women and babies. She knew very well how far from grace she had fallen. But what if she had succeeded? She could still wonder about that at the back of her wilful half-repentant heart. Half-repentant: repenting the consequences and not the cause, which is hardly a repentance at all.

For she still found it difficult to believe that man as he existed was the highest form of life. She still could not bring herself to see that because man questioned and concluded he was to be placed higher than animals who did not (to human knowledge) leave their doubts on death, on life, on gods, for posterity to ponder. She still found the very fact of man's arrogant will-to-know against him. Wild creatures contained their answer within themselves. They were complete unto themselves: their completeness was their answer.

The highest? Certainly the most stupid, the most destructive. No animal destroyed itself so willingly and so conscientiously as man. And yet the most afraid of death!

Uller had once told her that only two kinds of beings are indispensable: the peasant and the artist: the body and the soul: the bread and the wine. She was more and more inclined to the belief that only one of these was indispensable: the peasant, the body, the bread. Leave the drunken soul to its mischief; let it lie fallow a while and give bread and water a chance.

She could still think with distaste of mankind being born into a world not new and having to adapt itself to theories and habits made to fit it by others. How old, how nearly rotten with age seemed man's world. Hourly on its crust swarmed new life. New life appeared on the worn-out world and the worn-out world closed in.

And his children what were they? His challenge to Death. His defeat of death. His root which must not wither. His right to life by proxy. What he cannot achieve his children shall achieve. His work lies unfinished: never mind, his children shall bring it to completion. Safely, safely to completion. They were born only to bring to completion that which he had had to leave incomplete; and was presumably worth completing.

But she had not wanted, and did not want, to live by proxy. (Cook's Tourists in their own lives, had said Uller.) To her a child must be something complete within itself, without a why or a thank-you or a perhaps. She had asked of life a new form. A being who would have escaped the worn-out form and order of life. As other women ask deified parodies of their lovers or husbands; or like music and hope it will perform on a piano; or follow the family tradition of being a lawyer, a judge, a gentleman, a greengrocer; an engine-driver is the father merely a porter; a baronet is the paternal parent a mere industrialist. She still could find it strange that what man conceives in stone and colour and sound he cannot conceive in flesh and blood. So much for the drunken-soul of him!

Enough of the drunken-soul and its mischief. Out they rush with a wail into a worn-out world. The worn-out world closes in on the new life. And by the time the new life has freed itself (if it ever really does) it has acquired the prison garb and the prison habits. So that it cannot be free. It can never be free. Freedom is not for the new thing on the musty-smelling earth. The new thing will continue living its second nature. Always on its acquired habits.

She could still wonder at this at the back of her wilful half-repentant heart. That was the core of her. That was the drunken-soul core of her which she had plucked out and finished with at twenty-two; the mirage she could still see at times, though she no longer looked for it. For now she believed in the body and the bread. Wash child, wash corpse. Let man look to his own salvation. For woman it lay from the neck downward; breasts and thighs and pelvic bone. And for head the ever-enlarging heart. The fatty ever-noble heart swollen with appropriate emotions.

The darkness had not always been a menace to her. She had not always been afraid of going to his room at night. She had bent over him with becoming enough grace, as a child. But now he was no longer a child, and she had grown restless and tired and even rebellious. Not a little tired of it all.

It was now his turn to reproach her. She told herself that now that he was a man he reproached her, though she knew that he could no more do so now than on the day he was born. It was merely the morbid attitude of mind towards things large or small. Between killing a cat or an ox. The result is the same, but the one seems so much more unpleasant and brutal than the other.

She felt that everything had been repented of and in some measure expiated; and been turned to the calm that is or should be the reward of long habit and uneventfulness. And now it seemed as if the struggle must be taken up again, as though she had not finished it long ago and was entitled to her reward and rest. She had the right, she felt, to desire not to be disturbed.

So absorbed had she been in the years of attainment of her gradual peace that it had taken a dream to make her aware that he was a man. Uller told her that her son was now a man; and she had replied with that curious casual acceptance of dreams: yes, Richard is now a man. They were standing in the piazza and it was very hot. They stood together in heavy heat without shade. Uller kept looking over his shoulder with such persistence that she lost patience and said: one would say that your head was turned back to front. And Uller said: so it is. And so it was. So she went round to the back of him to talk. His face was not at all the face she remembered him to have had: but she knew his strong handsome hands which he now held joined as though in prayer as they talked. As they stood talking (she couldn't remember what was said) they became aware of Richard stalking them with an idiotic concentrated malice: darting about on the points of his toes from tree to tree and along the wall of the house opposite: focussing them with an awful intent with his long eyes, cool as water. They began fussing about in a sort of half-panic to avoid him and ran down a street leading off the piazza, dark with shadow. There he was at the bottom of it, waiting for them. They turned back and ran and ran and then she was in a carriage, an old enclosed carriage, something like an old London cab, which smelt rather unpleasant. She looked out of the window in the blinding light and saw that they were climbing a narrow steep path beside the sea, up and up a long rocky path. She was relieved. It was much too hot to run.

She heard some-one panting in her ears, although no one was in sight. Pant pant pant. Some-one was toiling after them, making a terrible effort in the sunshine to reach them. Higher and higher they climbed.

And then the coachman suddenly stopped for his horse's convenience. It went on and on; a fountain of horse inundating the road. The horse standing taut and slowly taking on the grey-green surface quality of stone. The coachman's back relaxed in a first attitude of sleep. This was awful. She leaned forward and with a weak hand shook the man's shoulder. His coat was so hot that she tore her hand away. The palm and fingers were lined with small white blisters; but she felt no pain. She opened her mouth to speak and her voice would not come; so she went quite close to the man's ear and seemed to pour her words in it with great and careful effort. Quickly, she said. We have no time to waste. Be quick. PLEASE BE VERY QUICK. She must be shouting now. She grinned at the ear, her mouth wide and set. I must be very gracious to him, she thought. She thought: now the road will be muddy and difficult to follow. He will slip and drown. And yet she knew that it was not so. Pant pant pant. The horse must be finding it difficult to climb the hill, she thought. And again she knew that it was not so. Her ears were filled with the heaving raucous breaths. He was gaining on them. Again she thought: it is the horse. And then felt the breath on her neck: a sudden hot jet running down her neck, thick and slimy. She shivered her head and turned to the window, and there was his face looking indescribably foolish and malignant, hardly larger than an apple, lolling to the right of the handle.

She was surprised, but not yet afraid. Then she saw that she was alone in the carriage and she thought: Hans has left me, and felt tears on her cheeks. Pant pant pant. The sound filled the carriage and with it the heavy dragging of feet. How tired he must be, she thought listening to the leaden dragging steps, and feeling an infinity of sadness for all who were tired. So much tiredness, she felt, saddened her. She wept a little, noiselessly, pleased that she could weep without noise.

And then quite slowly the head began to grow. It balanced itself on the projecting celluloid stick handle and with a fixed and horrible intensity grew steadily larger and larger. And as it grew she crouched. She found herself fighting to make herself smaller and flatten herself against the far side of the carriage to give it space. The panting became louder than ever and the feet dragged themselves with frightful, heavy menace. The head was now enormous: and as it swelled it slowly turned a nauseating purply brown colour. Its eyes were shut, but she felt that they saw her, had found out exactly where she crouched. And now she was frightened. She made a sudden agonising and futile effort to huddle out of sight. But by now the head had swollen to such dimensions that it filled the carriage window on all sides with its purply brown pulp. She smelt a sour decaying smell; a putrid smell of meat and excrement. She saw large drops of sweat oozing from the forehead and upper lip. It was swelling so rapidly that now it spread over the edges of the window and the frame gripped it painfully at the neck and skull as its colour darkened steadily. The windowframe creaked under the pressure of the monstrous swelling head which now took up more than half the carriage. Suddenly a look of indescribable agony came over its face; and then a sudden relief. And then without opening the eyes or relaxing a muscle, it quivered horribly at the window, wrenched itself free, heaved in a last supreme effort to reach her, and fell with a ghastly and deliberate clatter at her feet. She could not get them away in time and felt them wet and sticky with blood. And looking down at her feet she saw the eyes slowly open and look for her.

Lisetta was at her bedside. In the absurd kimono which she had discarded so many years ago. The silks frayed, the colours dead. Lisetta was holding her hand. Such screams! Mother of God, they froze the stomach. Ruth sat bathed in sweat. She clung to Lisetta's hand stupefied by the sudden light. She put up her hand to ease her hair away from her neck, and then at the ears and temples. At the roots it was wet and clotted.

Ho avuto un sogno. She ran her outstretched fingers through the wet roots of her hair, looking up at Lisetta so hardy and reassuring, smiling down at her a good reassuring grin of good-fellowship of the whole face; warming her slowly back to life. Non mi lasciare; non mi lasciare sola! Ho tanta paura. . . .

But Lisetta did leave her now that she was propped on her pillows, her hair newly brushed and plaited, to go to the kitchen and make some strong coffee. Ruth sat up, still and surprised, relaxed after the awful experience of the dream tension, and feeling physically weak.

It was nearly four o'clock. The sky was luminous with a fresh wash of pale colour; the dawn was breaking. She looked long at the sky which promised Lisetta so much. She sat still and surprised as though she had been rescued from sudden and brutal death. Rescued too late. She felt that she had died and been brought back to life. Late and unwillingly. Yet how good to lie back and take long looks around the familiar room, embracing it gratefully with the mind's eye, reassured and on the whole grateful, though physically weak as after a long illness.

Lisetta came back with the coffee and a dish of fruit. She said that Maria was afraid that she must be badly hurt to cry like that. Hurt? She thinks, explained Lisetta, that you fell out of bed. Which was just what was needed. She laughed till there were tears on her cheeks.

So that now she was obsessed with the thought that he reproached her. She knew that he could not do so, yet the obsession remained. More, it strengthened. How it came to her first she could not tell. It suddenly seemed right and natural that now that he was a man he should reproach her. So she grew restless and not a little tired of it all, feeling that she had paid, not in full, of course, but in great part. Almost enough. She did not want to begin again; how could she? She had been so intent on hoarding some measure of calm through the years which she voluntarily had dedicated to him. Now such calm was beginning to fail her, and she did not want to begin again. She had built up her calm of mind and body through twenty years and from much effort. It was a mistake, the years said, but it was long ago. It means little. It is forgotten. And here she was at the end of it all with her heart suddenly as feverish as a girl's; and no stronger.

In the immediate fervour of repentance following on what she had done, she had taken on herself the expiation of her sin. She had allowed no one to shoulder her burden for her: nor herself to shelve it. Which would not have been difficult, and far more pleasant. Cruel and selfish she had been. Had ridden rough-shod over everyone. They ceased once more to exist for her. The fervour of repentance was on her; she must expiate. And no one existed for her but her child and herself: herself only as an instrument of service. In such a state of mental fervour and will-to-sacrifice nothing could turn her from her purpose. She set and hardened to a state of maniacal rigidity of purpose, that daemonic rigidity of female purpose seen in female saints and poisoners. She could have passed through barred windows and iron-clamped doors. No prison had been devised that could hold her. She knew it and died to everything around her; lived only in the adamantine purpose of her female will.

She told Stephen the truth. That was part of the expiation, and his due. He did not believe her. How could he? I did this, she said. It is my fault. I willed it. I am responsible.

He was full of pity for her. His mind still could not compass the full extent of the misfortune that had suddenly come their way; and as though the thing in itself were not enough but she must needs take it thus. So she became cunning. Hard and cunning. Once her confession made she never again referred to her share in the matter. She let him think what he could not help thinking: exactly what they were all thinking. That this wild desire of hers to take the child away, abroad, anywhere, herself alone with it, her life given to it, was something rather sad and beautiful; was touching and beautiful. Wrong, ridiculous, but touching and beautiful. To be resisted as something which she would (must) eventually see when finally restored to health; when time had healed; for the unreasonable and useless thing it was. But in her heart she despised him. Despised his maudlin pity-offering: his gathering-together of all the sentiments proper to the occasion. All the correct gentlemanly sentiments which could most humiliate her in her pride; turning her fine courage to the delirium of a sick and disappointed woman.

As though she would be making this gift of herself to an accident! Was not this very desire for expiation the outcome of her guilt: and its proof? What had had accident to do with her? A fall? A throw back? A pre-natal impression. Would these have lighted the candle in her heart that not all the days of her life would put out? To how many women did that happen! How many children of good birth were to be found shut away in private homes, thrown aside, discarded in asylums; out of sight and mind and dutifully attended by all the comfort and neglect which money can buy. Could she not also have sent it away; placed it conveniently from sight; hidden it in the many rooms unused or seen; bought aid and ease for it and paid others to keep it from her sight for ever? Did they then find it so easy, this thing which she was doing, that she would do it for another's guilt?

Do not admit your guilt: cover it up, as a dog covers its dirt: let all be as it was. But she could not. She felt too deeply her share in the tragedy. Had the penalty been death she would have died. So she took her child away: ostensibly for a sufficient period of time in which to regain her health. But she knew she would not return. She left her Eden only too willingly; indeed had to struggle to get beyond the gates. She was surprised at Eve, hiding her face in her arms and weeping. The relief was immediate. She had been very hard and definite in her refusal to accept an allowance of money. This was her business. She had her small yearly income of a few hundreds; her own money; her father's money. It more than sufficed them. Outwardly she was numb. Nothing seemed to reach her. Her eyes remained bright and speechless.

Lisetta undressing him for the first time, unfolding the quiescent elegant bundle with the slow beautiful natural joy of the italian woman before the child, had given a high sudden cry, and Ruth had felt her heart tremble as she stood colouring with shame looking where Lisetta looked. The italian woman's sharp accusing cry as she stood with the small white sock in her hand: the soft first-shoe which some women lay secretly aside with a few toys and perhaps a letter or two. She had been told by one of the nurses that the child had come from her without a cry. That first lusty yell of relief a new-born creature gives at finding the struggle over, had not been given. He had made no sound. She remembered that now, and she was glad that she had left her safe Eden.

Had fought her way out of it to this sudden protesting cry. To the angry accusing cry which he had not been able to make and unknowing had found some-one to make for him. She was glad of it as she stood red with shame before the italian woman. But she did not expose herself again. She did not say: I did that. Never again. Not even to Uller did she say: I did that. He was puzzled as to whether it was a premature birth; or the result of an impression during pregnancy; or heredity; or an attempt at abortion: and rather favoured the last. She so evidently was not what is called a maternal woman. She showed little trace of affection for the child, though attentive to it in that she would sit beside it for hours on end and was restless until she knew with whom it was and where. She stitched away, embroidered, learned to knit, seemingly more to distract herself or pass the time away than because she was interested in what she was doing. He could never recall hearing her speak of it. Indeed there seemed to be some kind of tacit agreement among those about her that he was not to be mentioned.

Uller having suffered much from the maternal ardour of woman liked and approved her attitude, surprised that any woman could resist the temptation to impose her will with deadly and possessive female purpose on what morally and maternally and legally speaking was hers. He could not know that she felt no such temptation: having imposed her will.

He was nearly seven when Uller came to spend the June and July of 1913 on the island, and was still in the wheelbarrow-cum-bench-on-wheels of local manufacture and design. But later she ordered for him one of those gay painted wheeled carts from Castellamare: absurdly gay, primitive, and exotic with a profusion of reds and yellows, and a strangely-staring saint reliving his sad bright life about the panels.

What a char for my Bacchus, she thought grimly the first time she saw him seated in it, the children quarrelling among themselves as to who should push it on its first journey. She found that the wheels were too high, coming almost to the rim of the cart, and she was anxious (O exquisite irony) for his hands which he trailed over the sides; and the children came to learn that their first duty before starting was to see that his hands were inside the cart.

It seemed to her he had liked his new cart. He seemed never to tire of staring at the bright-coloured patterns. He liked bright colours. Any new bright pattern could hold his attention for hours. He would lie watching Uller at his easel with a catlike intensity of concentration, following the ladling on of colour (for to Ruth, used to the discretion of the English School which she admired, and the sobriety of the more soberly respectable Old Masters, Uller seemed to pat and plaster his colour on the canvas with a trowel. More like a master-mason than an academician, was her secret comment), and the movement of Uller's yellow-sleeved shirt. Uller had a circus-tent taste in shirts. Richard stared and stared and seemed to approve them. Any thing bright or shining he watched with the same feline intensity: and at times made sounds and sighs. Curious sounds they were, sometimes sharp and sudden, sometimes long and throaty: conveying whatever one read in them. But such, with that stare of hard concentration, that will-to-know look that came in his eyes, his brows drawn down and tense, that she would suddenly feel that only speech and movement were lacking, and that he was not. Not.

For instance his way of balancing himself on a chair and propelling himself strongly and safely about the terrazza. He had found that out for himself by accident. He was about seventeen at the time. While arranging the pillows and rugs on his painted cart they usually lifted him on to the bed or lowered him to the floor. For some reason this day, no bed being near, they placed him on a chair. His long legs touched the floor and swung against the chair legs. It was the first time he had ever been placed on a chair. In the unexpected freedom of his hanging legs he began, it seems, to rock his body. It was a slow hesitating movement without strength or consciousness. He rocked his body slowly and carefully. Then apparently gaining confidence he accelerated the movement, and with the gathering strength of the movement the chair began rocking also. All at once the chair moved forward slowly, jerking from side to side. Suddenly he stopped moving his legs; paused; and just as suddenly began again. He appeared to understand that the chair was moving at his will. At any rate he understood that the chair was moving. To the onlookers it was clear that he was willing it. The control came directly from his body: from the base of his spine and his back which were pressed against the back of the chair. Sitting there with his loosely hanging legs and stiffened back some sudden instinct of self-preservation seemed to be working in him. He swung his legs and stiffened his back and spine and the chair moved. He stopped: the chair stopped. So he moved on again.

They set up a clamour and a cry and ran to fetch her. A miracle! *Signor'* vien'—vien'-veder'. Un miracolo! Mother of God to have seen the day! And there he was stumping about the room on his chair: jerking slowly from side to side; the legs of the chair advancing slowly carefully, controlled by the mechanism of his spine and back. It was a strange and unreal sight. No wonder they thought it a miracle. It was so nearly a walk. It was as though by some divine dispensation he had been given the nerves, the spine, the haunch sinews of an acrobat, and the sudden decision and power to use them to advantage. His sense of balance alone was astonishing. The moment was tense with a certain macabre unreality and quite unforgettable. Herself in the centre of the doorway crowded with familiar figures whom in the excitement of the moment she could no longer distinguish, nor the many sounds and signs they made, watching avid open-mouthed this surprising acrobatic performance by something, by some-one who had not, to anyone's knowledge, sat upright in his life. A miracle indeed! How not? By what divine accident had he been placed this day on a chair instead of the usual bed or floor? What divine dispensation had come to his aid with the nerves and spine of an acrobat, and the sudden power to seize and use them? It was obvious and simple enough to be uncanny. Leave him, she said, to the exclamatory and awestruck household. Do not disturb him. Let him learn.

On and on he went. Rock, rock, left, right, this way, that way, advancing, retreating, avoiding, choosing his path. Slowly steadily monotonously surely. But how soon they had grown used to their miracle! By now they had almost forgotten that it had not always been so; such a familiar sight as he now was, rock-rocking his way about the house. He used it for all purposes, except for the sands or when the children went to the Pineta to gather pine needles or play, or went any distance from home and wanted to take him with them. Then they still used his painted cart, now in its third new coat, the same profusion of reds and yellows, the same tribulations of the same brightly staring saint on the panels.

No wonder she now felt that he reproached her his twenty-two years of uselessness. His one assertion of will his rock-rocking about the house; a blind vindictive man's stick beat-beating on the tiled floor for her ears.

Yesterday in the late afternoon on the point of going to the town she had come on him unexpectedly on the terrazza. With a swift preoccupied movement she came through the open doors. There he sat looking at nothing. The sudden unexpected movement must have frightened him for as she was about to pass he gave a high sudden laugh: like a shriek, a sob, a guffaw; something obscene and startling. She too was almost angrily startled. About to pass him she paused. She thought she detected something unusual, almost personal, almost angry in the sound, so unlike his usual shouts and noises. She stopped dead in front of him. Clearly her imagination was playing havoc with her nerves. However it was, she had the strong impression that it was not his usual cry. That he recognised her. She felt that he was speaking to her. So she stood quite still and on an impulse, thinking that it might please him, might reach him, she did a dreadful thing. She stood still and throwing back her face she imitated his cry, shrill and hollow and sustained: imitated it on the whole very convincingly. It was the first time she had ever done such a thing. Perhaps, she thought, I have found his way of speech. But the sound hung in the air too long. It laughed the last. It mocked her. Immediately it was made she knew that it was useless. The echo mocked her, leaving her ridiculous and shamed.

A look sly and alert came in his face. He listened. Obviously he was surprised. His mouth opened as though to make another of his sudden animal sounds, but he made none. Instead he gathered his forehead in a knot between his eyebrows, and his grey eyes, speechless, almost transparent, stared at her face, at her mouth, stared and stared from the one to the other with a wild surprised intensity. Was he waiting for her to repeat the sound? If he was she was incapable of doing so. Was it fear or menace in that fixed grotesque stare behind which he seemed to be gathering himself together to spring at her, or leap away?

She began to tremble slightly as she often found herself trembling in moments when he was not merely a thing dumb, pitiful, deformed, but something evil, monstrous, and unreal into whose power she had delivered herself. He knows! he knows! scrunched her feet over the stony path as she hurried away, going to the town the steeper and more tiring way rather than pass in front of him. Run away, scrunched her feet. Run away. Cain his own accuser. Whenever he stared full at her with that strained intense mesmeric look her heart trembled with the thought: he knows.

At such times had he suddenly spoken and accused her she would not have found it strange. She would have known even the words; she had been expecting them too long. She might even have been relieved. Which was absurd. He stared in exactly the same way at Lisetta, Pasquale, Maria, Concetta, the bowl of noci, the goats, the half-open door, the lizards on the evening walls, Mario plaiting his tight scarlet ropes of tomatoes, the mad high fiddling of the cicala, the crimson and emerald pepperoni lying about the tables, the wine-stained cloth, the coloured discs of the inlaid floor; any and every familiar sight of which, through some momentary trick of attention, he seemed suddenly aware for the first time.

He slept, and she was relieved and stood longer than usual looking down at his pale-coloured hair damp on his forehead, his curved eyelashes resting on his cheeks, soft eyelashes of a young and appealing woman; his well-cut nose, fine-nostrilled. Uller had once told her that she had the too-thin high nostrils of the fanatic. Richard had them also; asleep they gave his thin face a look of tension, almost of severity. His head thrown back on the pillow lay half out of the bed; his left shoulder lay across the edge of the bed; his left hand touched the floor. She did not lift him back for fear of waking him. But turned out the light and went out on the stone balcony that joined the house from end to end, and leaning on the stone edge of the balustrade wondered why strong and active beings are sad in sleep, nullified, emptied of all that which gives them reality, the husk of their own eagerness and pulsation: so that one cannot look on them asleep without pity; whereas weak and empty beings achieve in sleep a certain static unity, a borrowed strength, a certain three-dimensional reality that is not their own: as though in quiescence, in complete abandon, they were fulfilled, and serene and harmonious may no longer be pitied.

The moon lay sideways, effaced; a pale shell lying in ripples of blue sand. A wash of milky stars was on the dark surface of the sky. It was August, the month of shooting stars, often standing there she had counted as many as thirty within the hour, which reminded her always of Ibsen's remark on first seeing Milan Cathedral: the man who made that could make moons in his spare time and toss them into space! Below her the green vine-forest disappeared in a swaying movement of dark reeds waving darkly and tortuously on the floor of the sea and seen through heavy water. The heavy suction-sound of the sea was in it; sucking in, swallowing up, no traces left. Everything as it was; as though it had not been. It was like the dreadful sound of a bucket being thrown down into a well, a sound to which she still could not grow used. It was like death.

Strange that she should fear night who had no fear of death. Night fell so heavily, so inexorably on the earth: on her earth. How could one help fearing it? It was beyond all argument; beyond question. Nothing of this dark threatening-angel business about death. On the contrary it was clear-outlined and intelligible to her, just as night was dark and unreal to her. Night, like birth, was a wearisome, unfinished, repetitive business, whereas death was clean and final. She had not a particle of fear of death. And not because she expected some reward in a mythical hereafter. She found no comfort whatsoever in the many popular forms of belief in survival after death: so very much the coward's way out. The secret door one keeps ready.

Of course as a child she had seen Heaven as a vast very pretty mother-of-pearly domed hall, a sort of ducal ballroom magnified exceedingly, with golden gates and golden floors which would be slippery and difficult to walk on, though nice to slide on (but would one be allowed to slide on Heaven's floor?) and a great many carved and high-backed golden chairs with elderly people sitting on them; and at the end on a throne was God with his long grey beard (but very *very* kind to *every*-one), and the grey dove over his head and a great deal of golden light rayed from his head, and Jesus and his Mother and all the Disciples, and Latimer and Ridley and Sir Thomas More, and a great many plump Bishops and Deans and vicars and old ladies, and all the poor people now prettily dressed and smiling, and all the sick people now healed and pleased, and many beautiful angels and a great deal of music, and everyone singing; all the time singing and sitting very straight on golden chairs with high carved backs.

Followed inevitably the age when it seemed so much more real and worthy to go where all the wicked and interesting people went. The time when grew the suspicion that those glorious creatures, so passionate, or gay, or wise, or cruel, that the dun world could not forget them, deny them as it would!, would not have been at all at their ease among the Bishops and old ladies.

I t would be good to be buried under a tree, she had said, that after-noon on which they walked together above Barano. To be reborn each year in its sap and renewed in its bloom. That was the only form of perpetuity she could believe in.

One dies in a room, on a chair, on a bed, and one leaves a certain part of one's self in that chair or bed for ever. Nothing can ever wholly cleanse them of that influence: of what one has dissolved into. . . . Even when dismantled, broken up: there one is still in the bits and pieces: will always be. That is immortality. Manure the earth; fade out on the air. That is why it was so horrible going down to the earth in boxes. Not letting one have the earth and its action about one: coldly and tightly about one. It makes life so flippant, so negligible. To deny one's body to the earth and all that flows and flowers from it. Being respectable to the very end! The pretty box might keep the grave-worms out.

She could imagine if some-one she loved intensely came to die before her, burying them under a vine and each year when they flowered and came to fruition eating the grapes or having them pressed into wine. She said wine because everything is vine here in the South. But at home (why should she have said home? She corrected herself) in the North she would choose an apple or cherry tree. First the sharp staccato of new leaves and then those hard incredibly green buds, and then the morning on which one goes to the window, goes as though one were expecting nothing unusual, and it is as though the tree sang with steely blossom, so clean, so full of hope and promise, and then cherries like blood and rough apples like flesh. Of a person one loves that would be beautiful, she thought: for both. For the dead and for the living. I would like to flower and come again in the same way to the person who loved me sufficiently to want me to renew myself for them yearly. . . .

How strange and irrational we are, she said, going through an outworn symbol of drinking the blood of Christ whom we have never known; never fully understood or realised as a real person; who has been rather thrust upon one from childhood. A certain hallowed cannibalism. He had the right idea, of course. But only to the few. Only to the very few. Only to those who had known and loved him: and to whom he offered it. One could imagine him being very tired of it all when he thinks of the millions and millions . . . being thoroughly ashamed at having been made the refuge of the weak-minded. Or was it rather the weapon of the strong-minded?

Exactly. That he could understand. He felt like that whenever he saw a violinist or a singer or a pianist, or what they call a famous musician, bowing and scraping and thoroughly pleased with himself before the shouts and the thunder. He never looks around his audience to see their faces! He, Uller, wanted to jump on his chair and shout: Look at them first! Don't thank them till you've seen them! Had she noticed how musicians and priests get the most imbecile-looking audiences? Concert halls and churches filled with people with their mouths open and nothing behind their eyes but tear ducts? Why should Christ be more squeamish than Caruso or Paderewski? Judge a man by his friends! Then God be praised that an artist can't see his admirers!

And he was off and away chasing his musicians. How he loathed them all! And music. Especially Wagner. He called it Jew-sound. Thick and rich and unsimple. And if one ventured Scarlatti or Bach he said spinet-sound: a hammer on a nail and a piece of wire. He said music was a drug: as potent as religion and almost as pernicious. He called music auricular self-abuse. He said a singer or a violinist or a pianist was a well-trained acrobat without the acrobat's courage. He could perform without endangering his life. He could land on a wrong note without breaking his neck.

And their conceit! Was there a set of people in the world so eaten with conceit? The greatest painter alive hadn't the conceit of the smallest singer or meanest fiddler. And what was it all but a mixture of stubbornness and capacity to stay put. An unfair trick. A digital tongue-twister, as it were. A swim swan over the sea swim swan swim swim swan back to me well swum swan, in all its alphabetic variations, and when they had it pat they ran and declaimed it in public, and everyone thought it wo-o-nderful knowing how much sitting and tongue-twisting it had taken to achieve.

—I like my acrobats in pink tights and spangles, said Uller.

(Thoughts on death. . . . Wiser perhaps to keep such things to oneself.)

Priests and musicians: how he hated them! The two forms of drunkenness he hated most. What a relief to meet an honest drink-sodden man, decently drunk out of a glass!

—This from an artist.

But not a drunken one. He could explain the wherefore of each of his brush strokes. His compositions were mathematical problems correctly resolved. As clear and as difficult. Nothing drunken there.

Yet watch him at work with that mason's trowel of his. All that which to her was static, the stretch of hot white sea, the sands thick and heavy with heat, the cypresses hanging high above them in the cemetery, at the very edge of that formidable yellow rock once a moorish stronghold—static, dazed with heat, held erect and leaning on it: was to him nothing short of an eruption. His cypresses were agitated as a wave, wilful, tormented. Ugly, she thought.

—I do not see it like that, she once said, looking up from her book.

Apparently no one saw it like that or he would give up painting. Also, she did not see it at all. She, as indeed most people, saw only what she had been taught to see.

He never spoke to her of his work after once listening to her opinion. Not so much that she was a woman as that she was an englishwoman. It simply was not in the blood. How can the english appreciate art when they cannot appreciate women or food? You're wrong, he would say and turn away and the conversation was ended. His shoulders said Go away and don't annoy me, silly creature. Oh oh oh. She would walk away trembling at his insolence. She who had been thought unusually daring for her admiration of Whistler! *Whistler?* WHISTLER? Ought to have provoked a japanese war. International complications for botched spy-work! But you have Turner, you english. TURNER. Turner at seventy. What do you want with Whistler? Aren't there a hundred thousand Whistlers?

She had always thought that artists were gentle-spoken creatures, diffident, silent. She had once, shortly after her marriage, sat next to Mr Sargent at a small informal most-agreeable dinner-party, and had found him monosyllabic to the point of embarrassment. It was apparently his usual manner. And then dear Sir Edward Paston, with his white-maned Arthurian head, who had admired her profile and colouring so discreetly yet so warmly that there had been talk of sittings, but that they had left for the country almost immediately. How gentle and wise, how infinitely lovable he had been! Artists were gentle-spoken creatures, diffident silent. Those whom she remembered had been like that. She told him so.

Really, he was very patient with her.

With an uneasy tongue, parched and thirsty in its ceaseless promethean vigil, Vesuvius licked at the night air; its red tongue flickering, retiring, leaping hotly out again. An ugly thing by night Vesuvius. A dual personality if ever there was one. What a man thinks and what he says. The safe work-a-day world he creates for himself: the night world rising out of him in dreams from depths he dare not fathom. By day decorative and peaceful-seeming, receding in its waves of pale smoke into the blue crumpled background of the hilly coast. By night menacing and cruel: a man-made cruelty. Man-made in his own tortured image. A tentative hell. Probably an Inquisitorial toy left there by the dark-souled spaniards who knew so well the arts by which christianity could be turned to a Black Mass. The stench of its blood and smoke still rising to the night sky from its parched and restless throat. A flame on an altar on which a body lies, naked, mutilated, worshipped by the meek-old and men-women, and women women and women. Who must weep and fondle. And at its feet the ashes of what must have been, Athens excepted, the most exquisitely civilised and the loveliest city in the western world: sun-coloured, sun-fused, pagan. Tourists blister their feet on its pavements. The hire of a parasol costs three lire.   .

From far a thin sweet voice, young and pointed:

> cu' sti ccrucette d'oro
> e' sti rruselle 'mpietto. . . .

came drawn across the darkness like a fine chalk line across a blackboard

> nun date cchiú arricietto
> a chi ve vo' guardá!. . . .

and a woman's high nasal cry (every male on the island killed and every female from the age of ten given to the conquering spaniard, and Vittoria Colonna living on solitary splendour and occasional verse in the castel') a spanish voice curling upward from an open throat, rough wine from a wineskin: Giannin' . . . vien' . . . su . . . su . . . a' capit'? A door or window fastened noisily and abruptly.

From below, from somewhere at the back of the house, came the frightened scream of a child and then a long-drawn settled howl. One of the innumerable (innumerable-seeming though four in all) children of Lisetta's sister-in-law Giulia (Peppe probably), falling out of bed. As many as could be got in the bed and the least skilful falling out. Ask the reason for the cries the following morning and a gay shrugging: e Peppe . . . è cascato a terra. . . . Peppe's average was five falls a week.

There's your true peasant the world over. Knows the last farthing to be dug from the earth or pulled from the tree. But do not ask him to put that farthing on a mattress to keep his children from falling out of bed, no matter how much the earth and tree have yielded him. For God protects gli innocenti. The little innocents fall from bed and are never hurt. A grown man, yes. A man may be very gravely hurt in falling from bed: but never a little child. Why? How can one ask? Because God protects the innocent, Signora. The innocent may fall from bed:

God sees to it that they are not hurt. He may even push them out to show that they will not be hurt. For who would hurt a child, Signora? There she was sleeping between the wall and me . . . and there . . . right on her head, Signora. (Giovina jumps her small arms in the air, agitates her tiny hands, never meeting them though seemingly attempting to, and stares from her mother's arms with round pebbly eyes.)

Only the other day in Portici a baby fell out of a top-floor window (but you must have read of it too, Signora?) unhurt. Not even a bruise to mark the place it fell. For God protects the innocent. And if a man has children, Signora, God looks after him and he prospers.

He prospers. His children will work for him from the moment they can carry a bundle on their small heads or wield a stick on the ass's rump, or put up enough emulative noise to frighten it forward, or dig or fetch or carry or wash or spin or care-for or stand by to await orders. He prospers: and the woman in accepting the yearly child has found the means of keeping his favour and of being well treated and of being regarded as necessary. He prospers: for the more children the more unpaid servants: the more grandchildren the more security.

Five times of a morning under a fierce sun—she had caught herself counting them—had Maria taken her bone-thin nine-years-old legs the steep climb backwards and forwards on errands to the beach, the town, and up and down the flight of steps leading to the upper rooms with water-jugs and anything forgotten or suddenly remembered and immediately wanted. How immediately things were wanted! Mari . . . a. Mari . . . a . . . and her stubborn bit of tallowy face would emerge from nowhere and her bone-thin unwilling legs were on the stairs.

Going to her room the other day in the early afternoon she had found Maria squatting behind the door. Mari . . . a. Mari . . . a pealed through and around the house. Calling calling, angrily, persuasively, again angrily, impatiently, and cuckoo-pitched in various distances at once. But Maria continued squatting where she was found. Up went her finger to her lips. Not a pleading gesture but authoritative, severe, darkly menacing, her eyes very wide and black and stubborn. Such a flame of fury and defiance seemed to have burnt her to her bony brownness! A wiry angry dark little animal ready with nails and teeth. Only her brown feet were soft and gentle and childlike; such sad, tender feet with the beautiful even toes of the barefoot mediterranean child. Small bedouin in her one dusty garment. Black-streaked arab hair and beads of fine white lice on her black hair threads.

Twice Ruth had tried washing it: had brought her a brush and comb and parted it on this side; down the middle; combed it this way and that; put a bow here, taken it off there; plaited it in two thin whiplike plaits. And given it up in despair. The comb dug the earth; the brush had lost its handle when thrown at the stray dog seen near the chickens; the ropy hair hung again over Maria's eyes and the white beads gathered.

So she had had to give up trying to inculcate some sense of personal pride in her; talking to her of cleanliness, bribing her with gifts of coloured beads, a colour-bordered handkerchief, a little silver chained bracelet, and sweets. She had soon given up trying, and paid no more attention to her than to the other children. Yet she resented her failure. Had she been an english child she could have taught her to read or draw or play. She would have brought children's books and read to her; set her small tasks to puzzle over, if only for the sake of doing something with herself and amusing the child. But Maria was not amused. For days the child would avoid her, seemingly planning some subtle imaginary revenge; would snatch at the handkerchief or the beads with a nasty grin round her tight little mouth and make off round the nearest wall, still leering. Detached and defiant and all her own, her small savage heart unconquered.

And towards her Ruth alternated a complete indifference and intense exasperation. Little animal without soul! Towards herself contempt: was she seeking something to graft herself on, to possess? Why this thrusting of souls, of consciousness, on people and things? Maria remained detached and defiant and all her own; quite savage and contemptuous. A hateful child from a northern view. But she was right. O she was right. Cats have this same quality. Watch them walk away dark and ungettable for all the stroking and milk in the saucer. Monkeys have not this detached untouchable quality. They are merely mischievous in a sentimental way. Everything is written on their faces. But mediterranean children are not monkey children but cat children. Don't stroke them and you won't get scratched. So she left Maria to her one garment and beaded hair.

It had been the same when trying to teach (to her recurring shame) the first batch of children to say thank you. (That was many years ago. Nowadays she could hardly believe that there had been a time when she had found it necessary for a Forian child to say thank you when offered anything!) Keeping very near to the table in the hope of a fig or a slice of melon or a glass of wine with ice bobbing in it.

What do you say? Nothing. Snatch it and away and eat it out of sight and beyond recall. Yet with Giovanni she had persisted because he was sturdy and beautiful in his four years and months, and warmed through to an even brown and always naked; and also because beauty is hypnotic. Lisetta said that she put a shirt on Giovanni every morning but he was rarely anything but naked. Now and then he could be seen carrying something in his hand which looked like a shirt: carrying it at arm's-length. A compromise. It was wiser to let him strip himself. When told to keep his frock on he tore it straight up the front and there he was with two sleeves and two side flaps, as naked as ever and less comfortable.

Here you are, Giovanni: what do you say? Giovanni clutched at the cake and was stumping off but for a firm hand reached out to catch his arm in time. What do you say? And Giovanni would stand squarely planted and would stare at the cake, at the strange woman, at the sky, and finally say Signor' (which was doubtless what she had been expecting) and run off. Or he would say "Giovann'" that being a word he knew. He knew few words: and what did she want with him at all?

And once as he stood staring at her, straining to be off, Antonio his elder by three years, two enormous black eyes heavily lashed and lustrous, a narrow spanish face, thinly made, finely jointed and elegant as a young page (El Greco's son, Uller called him) as yellow and thin as Giovanni was baked and strongly planted, brought out in a snarl: ma ha *detto* buon giorno. He spat it at her. He *said* good day: now leave him alone. He was right, of course. The dark spot in the elder brother had found her out, snarling at her to leave alone that which did not belong to her and did not wish to.

How Uller had laughed and remarked on the activities of the english missionary service abroad! taking himself and his painting material off to the Pineta. She had watched him pass down through the vineyard with the naked taciturn Giovanni who clutched in his brown hand three fresh green figs, his little heels planted firmly in the dust. His brown serious strength made her sigh. He seemed to have grown gravely from the earth he planted himself on so securely and possessively. His small spine was like a rope of vine knotted and unbreakable. There was something of the same bloom and perfume on his skin as on an unpicked cluster of grapes. And strangely enough when Uller painted him—finally after the innumerable sketches he was always making—squatting there naked on the stones, he had painted him blue against the blue sky, among blue leaves, on blue stones. It was all quite absurd, of course; even ridiculous. No one was blue; a sky might be, but leaves were green and stones were grey and the naked child was brown. And yet for all its absurdity he had caught the browny-blue bloom which Giovanni gave off like a fruit, even though he had painted him bluer than the skyey background, or any sky that ever shone for that matter. Was it blue or purple? Still more unusual, Uller had declared himself satisfied with the work.

Now both Antonio and Giovanni were in America: had been for the last ten years and were sending money home as would their children and grandchildren: for God prospers the man with many children. Prospers him especially if they are in the americas. It was everywhere on the island the same. Not a family but had a son in the americas or one ready to go or one preparing to go as soon as his military service was done with. All were going. All were preparing to go. All were eating their hearts out because they could not go. Everywhere notices of steamship sailings and snatches of american-english. For they returned and built large ungainly villas and were called americanos.

Now everything wanted was called for partly from heaven but largely from America. At Piedimonti the church of Monte Vergine was being almost entirely rebuilt after having been in a state of dangerous decay for years. The glittering campanile new-tiled; new bells cast and clattering. Heaven had been warned about it for more years than were counted, but it was not until some devout mind remembered the americas that anything was done about it. Now the money was being sent home to mother weekly from every son of the parish and the Madonna had as steady and proud a house as she could wish for.

When that old brigand Mazzello returned from America with the proceeds of his rum-running activities and bought the handsome green-and-red-painted barca—which can be seen any day in the porto laden with its wine barrels and onions and melons for the peaceful and sleepy trip from Naples to Foria Ponte, though sometimes going as far afield as Livorno—he flew the american flag in gratitude. And there it waves symbol of good fortune and plenty, the envy and admiration of all. A man may return to his own country but his heart remains where his money was made.

And the corruption was everywhere. The malignant cancer which decays and lops off a man from his earth, and for which there is no cure. Stony ground where forests stood and sandy wastes where was pasture land and fruit-bearing trees. The uprooted gaining clean and useless hands and neat town-grey faces.

Once when she had questioned his curled seas and tormented trees and strangely-limbed-and-coloured children, Uller had said: Unless a thing is three times removed from nature it is not art.

Be that as it might. Certainly a man three times removed from nature was no longer a man. And they were all doing it. Removing themselves from the earth unto the third generation, and the lunacy and childbed-death statistic beings visited on them as a form of removal tax. Going into shops and workrooms and the envied few returning with dollar-conscious grins round their mouths and littering the country with ugly villas, smugly entrenched behind the envied title of americanos.

Had not he himself said: in another year or so I shall go to America. Either of them. Preferably South. Europe is dying, already gangrened and fly-blown. A decaying deposit of century on century.

It told on him being born to the somnolence of a canal-gazing, bier-halle, Ritter und Thurm, timbered house lurching against timbered house in the unsober medieval picturesqueness of Strasbourg. He said: a house built especially for oneself is better than an old house built for others and in which one is compelled to live. It may be the same with countries. Anyway, in a couple of years when he had put together enough work he'd find it out for himself. And whatever he was to find, he said, it would not be a corpse.

Of course the sun had really done more for her than anything else. Much that she attributed to time or habit or to her own inner struggle was the sun seeking her out, dissolving the darkness, the sense of doom and guilt that was like a poisonous drug of slow action. She told herself not without bitterness: I seem born to hide. But the sun did a great deal for her in searching her out and extracting the poison and dissolving the dark anger-spots. Before the sun's strength the action of her willed bitterness was powerless. Doing for her what Uller had said electric light was doing for the world; flooding the dark corners; turning the brave light of reason on the over-accumulated and over-revered débris of centuries. In time she came to lie back and watch it all, and in the light of the sun to see much not formerly visible; although she was dead and did not really belong and seemed to be resting there: a stage on a journey she was never conscious of desiring to complete; and which taken all in all could be only death. An unusual woman; taking little interest in the company in the thoughts in the doings of other people. She was restless now because he reproached her and seemed to menace her, so that it all came back to her again the first sense of guilt and shame. Much of it the result of living alone with him for so long. Perhaps, she thought, it is because there is no one whom I love. But who was there for her to love? She did not love easily, and he whom she had loved had left her years and years ago, and she had lost masses of her beautiful and shadowy hair, and had married without really wanting to but because a woman needs warmth and a fireside and protection.

And the action of the sun went on and on. She had been bitter and unhappy, though perhaps not altogether as bitter and as unhappy as she believed herself to have been. Who is? And she had gained quiet and a certain measure of satisfaction. Mostly the action of the sun on the skin, and intense blue light of sea and sky on the eye: though she put it down to an inner struggle that was perhaps a little more Laocoönean in retrospect than it had been. In the sunlight black spots dissolve in the consciousness as before the eyes. In the sun the struggle and the chaos adjust themselves in sleep. Take from a cold climate a man intending to commit suicide and place him in the sun and the intention will be sublimated to a quiescent fatalism. In the light of the sun it simply isn't worth it. (In which one gains the doubtful advantage of being numb without being dead.)

At first it had taken her by surprise. She had never imagined that a sun could be so hot nor shine so long; nor skies be so enduringly blue and cloudless. Her eyes ached alarmingly. Her head hurt with attacks of mild sunstroke from the reflected light. She felt like a candle in the sun, wilted, grew white-faced and scarcely touched her food.

The Hour of the Damned Souls, the name by which the natives knew the early hours of the afternoon, she found no exaggeration. Everywhere the heavy powdery dust lifting in clouds only to settle more greyly and heavily. Flowery grey dust in the bushy hair of the islanders: hair rayed from low foreheads in wiry bushes and held down by a thread of osier root so as to free the eyes: as with the youths in the greek statuary where it is mistaken for beauty or effeminacy, and is mere utility. Warm grey dust on everything. Grey-powdered feet; eyelashes grey with dust; grey vines; grey cacti; grey carts; grey leaves; grey dust smeared thickly on the billowing road-bordering walls in which the small stones rose and fell in cobbled rhythm.

Everywhere flies in angular flight. Restless dogs worried by flies. The hammer hammer hammer of asses and mules kicking the cobbles. The long white dusty roads that ate at the eyes, and walls glowing in the heat like naked sword-blades held to the eyes. Splayed green leaves luminous against the sky. All form all colour petrified in the brasier-glow of intense light. Fig trees hanging their long flat hands in purple shadows. Stone-coloured lizards motionless on lizard-coloured stones.

And never a soul in sight. On the spangled surface of the sea a sail leaning toward its phantom self. At this hour she was not so much alone as lying above the world in the detached isolation of an island; mind-less before the tranced Blakeian unreality of lying in island space and mattering not at all. Lost on the rim of a crater; on the small upthrust-ledge of volcanic rock. At any moment thrust down again to the floor of the sea. As far as sight could reach only the steely setting of blue water and the tranced passionless suspension between heaven and earth.

N eedless to say, singly and in groups and on whatever pretext offered itself all the de Chiara offshoots and their friends had descended on Lisetta to have their look at her; and having stared care-fully and well, and decided that it was sad to be mad so young and asked Lisetta whether she had any religion, the women peered at the sleeping boy and professed themselves astonished at every detail of its infant face; and went away with exasperation in their hearts, envying Lisetta her windfall. Having a mad foreign woman in the house was equivalent to having three sons in the americas: three sons doing well.

She had allowed herself to be stared at and commented upon, both because she could not stop them doing so, and because she had no feel-ings on the matter. It was Lisetta's triumph and it was difficult to grudge her her evident pleasure in being questioned and cross-questioned and sending them away half-answered; their heads full of difficult arith-metic and comparisons between hard work and the ease of having a mad foreigner on one's hands for life.

She listened and understood scarcely a word. Except that once hearing the words fiasco di vino she had become red and hot and moved away thinking that they had called her child a divine fiasco, instead of innocently calling for another bottle of wine.

But now from having lived among them long she had become almost a legend and quite negligible. Recently taking her afternoon siesta as usual on the veranda alcove facing her room she had seen a group of tourists staring up at her and pointing her out among themselves. They had evidently come especially from the porto to have their look at her. It was Giulia. She knew it. Giulia, Lisetta's sister-in-law, eternally the war-widow, eternally-the-mother, loathing her charity and despising herself and its donors, attaching herself to it like a leech; servile and arrogant and entrenched; two large unsteady melons stuffed in the front and the back of her; and arms and legs of equal thickness. One of those heavy yellowish-white women whom the lithe arabs prize so highly, and Naples and the coast abound in.

For the first time in all their years together Ruth spoke angrily to Lisetta. But she was not a tourist attraction. She was not one of the sights of the island. And having been turned into one she would leave the island as soon as her packing was finished. But Lisetta with a clatter of words and upraised hands was angrier still. Her nursling, her turtle dove, the english signora had been offended. She knew who was to blame. And on and on the two women clattered at each other in the kitchen, their voices pitched to the high grinding of an unoiled axle of an old cart-wheel. Giulia denying, admitting, cajoling, menacing, losing control of the bile stored in years of real and imaginary humiliation, calling on her children to prepare to tramp the roads and beg their bread now that they were homeless, foodless, without pillows for their heads or covering of any sort, for God is on the side of the rich and arrogant and has no pity for the widow and her fatherless children; and having worked the children up to various degrees of tears and variously pitched howls, burst into tears herself, calling and sobbing and rolling her eyes upwards and round, her tightly buttoned melons heaving perilously. Of course there were apologies and appeals and absurdly dramatic and biblical references to fatherless and starving little ones. Poor Giulia had had a shock. She had accused Lisetta of putting a strange woman before her own flesh and blood; of being more fond of her than of her own family. Which was probably much more true than ever Giulia in her anger realised, and certainly was not the safe appeal the widow had hoped. Perhaps Lisetta would as soon have turned her own daughters out of doors as seen Ruth go. Doubtless a judicious blending of affection and interest: but on the whole affection uppermost. Lisetta liked having her about; liked looking at her; liked looking up at her. Found her pleasure in serving her. Why or how she could not say: her need was stronger than any reason she could give for it. Her mad one had become indispensable to her. Giulia certainly had had a shock.

But Andrea, brother of Lisetta's husband, Mario, was altogether a delight. Ruth took Uller up to see him, right up beyond the Pilastri to the grey arab house with the worn outer stairway leading to the first floor and flat roof: within the room so dark that one asked if a prison were more forbidding. And in one corner of the long room where a table was vaguely outlined with a few plates and mugs, and a narrow barred opening high up in the wall filtering her some rays of light, Amalia his eldest daughter sat working at the loom day in day out and one wondered how she knew when it was night.

There was Andrea fixing the rat traps among his vines, shirtless, his trousers belted low on his thighs, balancing himself on his heels, walking with the roll of his thighs and buttocks like a small and friendly ape. All around him among the vines and fruit trees dodged his eight, or was it twelve?, children (one was always meeting another of Andrea's children) making of his paternity a gypsy encampment, gypsy-coloured, gypsy-garmented, barefooted and shy as wood creatures. From a distance they trailed after their father, stalking him.

He, back on his heels, laughed and talked and mimed and explained: the one person on the island except Lisetta who laughed from the heart and not the teeth, she always thought. Andrea was lively and mischievous and turning grey; a reddish gleam in his brown skin and grey-marbled eyes. He took them round to see the new traps and the gun placed in position over the water-cistern, full of his grievance against his rats, and the damage they were causing, and, of course, the further taxes on wine and the lack of last winter's frost. If only the brutes (and this year they were twice as large as any rabbit he had ever known!) would only content themselves with one bunch and have done with it: but no, they must go from one to the other nibbling, nibbling. No rat gnawed more than one grape from a cluster but picked and chose and ruined as many as he could, which was pleasant if they were your grapes.

Taking a handful of nuts from his pocket he cracked them between his teeth and held them out to them; and then Ruth made him take Uller to the corner of the vineyard where in an egyptian tomb of a square stone hut were the two long deep stone cisterns, vast stone troughs where the men trod the grapes, leaping in up to the armpits in a frenzy of sweat and singing. The women having brought the grapes in the long plaited baskets, watching and singing but taking no active part in it all. You couldn't let a woman tread the grapes or the wine would be sour and unsaleable. Why? Because it always had been so: who would drink wine that a woman trod? Andrea spat. It was a man's job and a man's drink. Not that there was much music and festa about the business now; it was just a work to be done and done well and quickly. But there had been a time, long years ago, in his youth, when it was a matter for frenzy and wild music and songs sung that were heard only on that day of the year, and the zampognari came and there was more feasting and laughter than at a dozen weddings. But now the youths of the place were a poor lot; the flower of them scattered on the mainland and in foreign cities. And taking a jug which stood under one of the enormous barrels, Andrea watched the yellow cloudy liquid pour in, took it in his hands, drank some himself first, and then handed the jug to Uller, who offered it first to Ruth, who saw the amazement in Andrea's round eye, knew what it meant and wouldn't have hurt his phallic pride for the world; and made Uller drink first and drank after him, though properly she should have passed it on to Domenicos, Andrea's son-in-law who stood by and the two men workers and then to the several male children: after which she came and the female children.

Up went the jug, child after child dipping its face in the opening and tilting it backwards. First thing in the morning before going to work with father, they drank the yellow clouded wine with their piece of earth-coloured bread broken from the loaf and stuffed with garlic. Drank the very dew from heaven where squeamish pale-faced youngsters the world over dipped their delicate noses in glasses of cold milk: cow-juice v. sun essence. And Andrea balanced on his heels, his hands in his belt called attention to himself as an example of wine-drinker: mother's-milk and wine the only liquids he'd known in his life, and was there a man like him on the island, or a hundred miles along the coast either way? Leaning back on his heels he rubbed his furred chest as though pleased with the feel of himself, and placed a hand on the matted, tasselled hair of his youngest child.

Mario, on the other hand, spoke little and shared the dark untouchable quality of the island soul. He would sit silent and shut-in seeming, plaiting his long scarlet garlands of small scarlet tomatoes which were hung like beautiful blood offerings on the walls of the house and about the poles which held the vine-trellis over the ristorante. Watching him hang his garlands with a care that was almost reverence was like surprising Abel preparing the first sacrificial fruit offerings for his altar. Mario's face was mapped and leathery, his eyes expressing nothing. He was a good twenty years older than Lisetta. Nor she nor his children paid him much attention. He was there and he was theirs; still useful in his way, though wracked with rheumatism.

Every morning after first standing up to his knees in the sea, motionless, pipe in mouth, he dug himself in the hot yellow sand. There he lay, umbrella over his head, pipe in mouth, packed in sand to his thighs, his trousers beside him in the shade; and after an hour's baking of his bones he would dig himself out, brush the silky sand from his legs, get into his trousers with a furtive peasant modesty and climb back for his midday food and drink.

Mule-stubborn to the pitch of exasperation. It was he who placed the poisoned leaves among the vines for the rats:. and the rabbits died. Again and again and again; poison for the rats and dead rabbits. And he wouldn't see it. It was his land and he could place poison for the rats where and how he chose.

The one person he seemed to take any direct interest in or care much about was Nicola, his son-in-law. Each evening they played cards together against the other men while Pasquale sat watching from a near chair, sulking with that sulkiness of old men aware that they have outstayed their welcome; hanging his toothless stubbled head and mumbling now and then some remark which no one could make out, or troubled to.

Staring past Graziella bringing the wine would move the very old man to remark on women. His own, he said, it had lasted him fifty-five years. A good woman while it lasted. But dead now a long time. Femina always dies first. She worries with the children and suffers much.

N icola under a tree peppering away in the air with a dreary intensity. One solitary bird on the island and he must be after it. Padre Antonio bending with heavy effort over Maria's waxen image says that little girls who cannot place a hand on their rosaries at a moment's notice are not regarded with much favour in heaven.

Poor man he might as well have spared his breath and the effort it cost him doubling himself to fix Maria sternly with his solemn black ink-spots; globulous, not over-clean. Once around the corner: the back of the hand jerked three times from under her chin and her mouth pursed to a button. That was Maria's opinion of that. The gesture clearly a trifle exaggerated in a desire to impress the Signora but on the whole expressive of her opinion of him. To be screamed at and boxed soundly on the ears she understood; but to be bent over and have a few unsubstantiated threats breathed on her face deserved the contempt it met with.

About him to Ruth there lingered always the flavour of Uller's contempt. How Uller had disliked the man on sight! His heavy-lipped pendulous face and fatty well-being. Reminded him, he said, of his moneylender in Paris. God's beetle. How he had baited the poor man and been inexcusably rude and harsh to him, seizing any pretext to insult him with a pleasure bordering on viciousness. It came to such a pass that Padre Antonio could not bend down to pat Giovanni's cheek without prompting a loud aside: Another male saint mauling a small child!

And when the priest (feeling it his duty to come to grips with the unbeliever, the foreign devil sent to tempt himself and corrupt those he guarded) had expounded and held forth and made all his known and narrow defence of faith and human aspiration, Uller would bring his fist on the table and tuning his voice to deliberate resonance and invitation, would ask: What faith? What perfection? And who decreed that man should be other than what he was? A few inspired minds at intervals of centuries had seen him clearly for the low animal he is and is meant to be. And had refused to believe it. So they assumed that he must know it himself and desire to be bettered. Rubbish. A man has certain functions to perform—and so long as he performs them adequately he is alive.

—The indictment, said Uller, came from Christ Himself: feed my sheep.

A sound judgment, that. As good as anything Solomon ever said. If He had no illusions, Padre, why have you? But personally, much as he admired Christ for much sound sense, on the whole he preferred Buddha. If only that he had no father waiting for him in heaven. God! how sick he was of people with fathers waiting to shoulder their burdens and kill calves and make life generally warm and saltless!

Besides, christianity had been too long used as a political weapon and as such must perish. How long, O Lord, how long before the people outgrew their priests and caught-up their great men? The few who came to them with messages which they read three hundred years later and said with bated breath: The genius! The forerunner! Centuries ahead of his time!

Stuff and nonsense and be damned. No great man had ever been ahead of his time: his time had always been behind its great men. His Time had always, like Savonarola's Army of Innocents, gathered in his inventions of the devil and his printed heresies and his lewd pictures and burned them on the little bonfire which they assumed was Oblivion.

And walking to the shutters he flung them open releasing the hot radiant light which poured out into the darkened room in a shower of golddust, and shaking his fist at the sky bellowed: There is our true god, my dear Padre. And when *he* dies you may be quite sure we die with him.

The priest had departed chewing his lips. And Uller watching him from sight had hopped up and down in front of the window like a large ruddy baboon.

—You make yourself ridiculous teasing the unfortunate man, she had said, thinking kindly of the priest's distorted face. And to no effect. Why don't you throw stones like a schoolboy or stand behind the door and jump out on him?

—I will, said Uller, he'd understand that.

And with faith so with human conduct. Bringing his light to a blind man. Showering wisdom on this fool. Then leave him to himself, said Ruth, he does you no harm. But no: he must demolish, tear down, drop the bottom out of the man's world; though he could have spared the energy he put to it. His victim was secure: what was not writ in his breviary: was not.

Marriage. One would have thought that Padre Antonio had invented it, patented it, and popularised it.

—The Church, which lives on the people, and the State, which lives from the people, encourage a man to marry. A married man is a slave. He is a man in chains. You have him where you want him. He is easily punishable. He is good. He is docile. He will not easily leave his children. The State has perfect control over the married man. Should he revolt, his wife, his children, his field, his house are his hostages to the State. In him also the State has four or five potential soldiers: and no responsibility.

Marriage enslaves the man: but his slavery is perhaps less heavy to bear than the slavery of the woman. (Ruth settling back, smiled. She at any rate could listen to him with malicious pleasure.)

—Women are not virtuous. They are by nature more lascivious and uncontrolled than men. (Padre Antonio raised shoulders and hands as though the chastity of the Blessed Virgin Herself had been in question.) Now when a man is given the right over a woman by the State and the Church he has the right and power to keep that woman in slavery. No man may approach her. She may go nowhere without his sanction and knowledge and in a few years her youth and desirability are past. The woman has been destroyed: the man's freedom has been destroyed. But it is doubly hard on the woman.

—A brothel protected by the State suffices for the man. He need not sin. He may not want to. But the fact remains that he may should he want to. He has, therefore, mental freedom. He knows that should he desire he may gratify. This mental satisfaction gives him an illusion of freedom. Meanwhile the woman has been several times blown out like a balloon: nobody desires or covets her. She has neither mental nor physical freedom. She is either carrying a child inside her or children are clinging to her skirts. No man can desire physically a woman large with child. Except to the artist a woman with her belly magnificently full is not a thing of beauty. Even you will admit, Padre, that a woman large with child is hardly an aphrodisiac.

The priest's eyes narrowed; how he hated the man!

—You may say that she may be unfaithful to her husband if she chooses. But the curious thing is that she rarely chooses. I speak of the average man and average woman. In fiction, yes. But it is extraordinarily difficult in life to find a woman who is unfaithful to her husband, or wants to be. On the contrary she is viciously, narrowly and furiously faithful to him. And by the time she has decided to be unfaithful, neglected and unable to please him, she is not wanted by other men.

—Always the people run for the State rather than the State for the people. The Church and the State. The Few: devising their splendid sacred laws to keep the rabble tamed. The Church-State the owner; the shepherd counting his sheep, feeding them, protecting them until the time comes for slaughtering them. So don't talk, Padre, about the godhead in man as though man had anything to attain or could be bettered. A man has certain functions to perform and as long as he performs them adequately he is alive. No more and no less. Christ called them sheep. They were sheep before he noticed it. They are the same sheep today.

Uller said that the root of the slavery of mankind was marriage.

And it never occurred to the baited priest, woman without woman-wit, to assure his lecturer a little pointedly that he spoke as a married man. Even as a much-married man. Which it was obvious that he was, loathing his wife and loving his two children. Or having loved them once. Now in a sense they were no longer his. A man's children are his own for so short a time. And he saw them rarely. At most once in two years; and each time they became more and more like two bright strange birds settling a moment on his hand or shoulder and flying unconcernedly away.

Again and again he spoke to her of his children. His face would grow hot with the strain of a certain comic innocence and fun. He would forget that he had told her the story several times; and each time had told it with the same precision, the same emphasis, the same surprise and the same laughter, in which the father assured himself that he had once had children. So she would stand with him again beside the goldfish bowl under which his youngest child had stood and called: O father, come quick and see! They are waving their little hands!

But it was the stories of his eldest child whom he had tried to teach to draw which pleased him most. Who when given a bell to copy would draw in the tongue. Why? Because it was there inside. But one could not see it. No: but it was there and if it was not drawn the bell could not ring. The same with a cup of flowers: drawing them inside the cup, on its face, as it were, and not growing from out its rim as they should have been. And asked the reason he argued that the flowers were inside in the water, and that if you drew them out they were no longer in the cup but in the air, and that could not be. And if given a box with lettering or a design on it to copy he would draw the box neat and bare and place the lettering or design apart, beside the box. Why? Because otherwise people would think the lettering or design was shut-up inside the box, which would be quite wrong.

You see how right he was? You see the clear rational workings of a child's mind? Extraordinary. Extraordinary. And only just five.

And one day he had taken a sheet of paper to draw where his house stood, and said: And then you come to the end here and you go down a long road; and had drawn with much care one long wriggley line right across the page. O but it is a much longer road than that, isn't it father? May I have another sheet of paper? And you go on and on down the road. Another line drawn with much care and anything but straight right to the very edge of the paper. O but we haven't come to the house yet! Another sheet of paper, another slow careful line: and still not there yet. What an interminable road it must have seemed to the small Johann! Six more sheets of paper before he finally reached home; and when he got there it had become larger than a church with a belfry and a bell, and a stork wheel to top it all.

And one day the child had come to him and said: Father please open your mouth . . . wider . . . still wider. I want to see your heart.

Beside the dark effaced islanders Uller was like a fistful of straw held to the sun. And it was just that pale luminous solid-fleshed german-curved thigh and buttock quality that one was not sure of; so inefficient seeming beside the subtly jointed bone-thin effortless strength of the small island men. Instead of turning brown he blistered red; in itself discordant and comic, and giving his easy-going blond largeness an air of a well-fed prize entrant at a baby show. But, as he said himself, he had it under the hat. His mental outlook his father's, a French-Alsatian, whom he had lost when he was ten years old. His bones and colouring those of his square heavy-breasted german mother who had wanted him for the priesthood; who had beaten and bruised him with her fleshy boxer fists; who had broken and ground down those first packets of coloured chalk bought after weeks of planning; who had burned his first drawings before his eyes, holding him down by the neck like a rat, like a house dog that has misbehaved on the mat; who from his store of memories made him once describe the navel cord as more deadly than the hangman's rope.

He said things which in her world simply were not said, were not thought: but she had lived too long out of any world to care what was said or thought. And it was exactly in this that he was new and stimulating and stood for something she had never known in an atmosphere of narrow gentility and insularity which is so dully and ineradicably County and the Services; and to which she had been a rebel, the stimulus of her father ever uppermost in her mind. In which sense Uller pleasantly was not a gentleman: having come to his own conclusions: having tramped most of Europe's capitals since the day of his sixteenth birthday on which he walked from his home and slept in their doorways; stayed behind when the others left to gulp the worked and charcoaled bread left on their easels and steal whatever lay about, choosing always, with youth's justice, the overstocked boxes of the wealthier students, here a brush, there a tube of paint; having grown skilled in the many devices whereby such necessities as drink, food and women can be had at another's expense; finding the world a decent enough place on receiving the charity of a few francs for his canvases; having risen by such steps to the notoriety of a few art-show scandals to the privilege of having the discerning Brothers Grünheim store away his canvases in their Paris cellars against the possibility of his early death.

And so here she was after all these years repeating his words; still pondering much that he had told her. Was it then true after all that women were but the receptacles for man's thought and children? Only that which he placed within her could be hers; her consciousness and life derived only from him. An acrid-tasting pill. Yet here she was still conscious of him; still finding her pleasure in remembering and repeating him and giving him shadowy life beside her.

He had never explained, or shown diffidence, or understood that there were things which one does not discuss; and which troubled her. As when he told her that his sister was the first woman he had loved. One day he saw his mother beat her, striking her heavily across the face and head, and heard her cry out. And all at once he loved her. Love came up in him like sudden tears. Passionate love, making him aware of himself. For many years he could not believe that there lived anyone more beautiful, more dear, than this girl who had their father's long gentle face and calm movements. She had nursed him through a schoolboy attack of chicken-pox. It remained one of the happiest memories of his life. How he had tried to become ill again! Calling on boys who were said to have measles: taking off his coat in winter to catch cold. Alas, he had his mother's bones and death-defying constitution!

When the time came he confided to her his plans of escape; but she would not come with him to Paris. She did not share his need to see the rest of the world. She cried; she feared for him; but she did not try to restrain him. His first lesson in womanly caution. He was shocked, but he forgave her once he got to Paris and the problems of art and food engrossed him. The day he became rich and famous he would go back and fetch her; not knowing that when next he saw her they would be married to different people; she absorbed in her first child, a boy whom she called Hans, and very sisterly and benign. Yet even today he would become excited and happy as a schoolboy at the thought that he was to see her soon. And this though she understood him not at all. Not at all. Found him strange and restless and not altogether a family asset. It troubled Ruth; but the story of the drowning man pleased and excited her.

As a boy he was standing on the bridge near the washerwomen's floats, near the Quai St Jean, as one comes up the road from the Grande Rue, gazing down into the water, when he realised that what he had at first mistaken for a dog or a piece of driftwood was a man going down for the second time. Appalled he threw off his coat and flung his leg over the bridge to leap after him. He was a strong swimmer. Yet just as he hoisted himself to the bridge to bring over his other leg he thought: suppose this man does not want to be rescued? And he sat there and thought it out. In a flash, as one thinks at such moments. He was only fifteen at the time but thoughts of suicide were not new to him and here was an unhappy man. A man doing what he had sometimes thought of doing. He remembered thinking: Perhaps, poor fellow, he had only just so much courage. If I rescue him he may not dare again, and I shall have his misery on my soul. So instead of leaping in he sat and waited for the drowning man to reappear. And when he did he must have guessed the boy's thoughts for he nodded; showed his teeth in a smile; waved a feeble hand and went down. The boy put on his coat and went home, smiling also.

He was amused at her attitude.

—Women as a rule loathe the story: and loathe me ever after.

But she liked it; liked its power and ruthlessness. It was good to let die a man who chose to die. Good to let people go their own way with a male remorselessness beyond female comprehension and pity. She liked it and it frightened her. It was just in that that he was a stranger to her. That woman-what-have-I-to-do-with-thee? male impersonality. In women it was different. Then when she would expect him at the beach, at the Pineta for the walk or picnic they had agreed on the day before, and he did not come and had forgotten utterly, she would know that it was deliberate. That it was calculated. Women forget nothing: they act only deliberately. But with him it was indifference: to her, to time, to common courtesy. Something impersonal to which she could not reach. And which shocked her more, for a woman is most shocked by the impersonal. That appalling male indifference which means simply indifference. That she could not cope with.

But woman, as he said, was but one need. It was not true that woman was man's most urgent need. In civilisation there is no hunger and no fear as it was first understood. Therefore woman happens to be the need nearest to us and we can take advantage of it.

Woman (he said) was but a limited influence in a man's life. Of course there was mother-love and patriotism which in the patriotic figurehead was always (had she noticed?) a brawny, open-mouthed, shouting woman in whom men saw again the bullying wife or mother: so that they were hypnotised into obeying: collectively awed by the presence of this open-mouthed arm-raised female; and marriage.

Yet when a man looked back on his life to count its pleasant interludes, his memory lighted first of all on his school and student days and the solitary years of his early struggles: periods when, shaping himself, he lived his own male life beyond and outside woman's influence. Perhaps the only free days a man lived. In that hour, beyond wife or mother or child or mistress, a man would choose his friend as having given him the more complete and lasting satisfaction: the give and take of free human intercourse, which is not between man and woman.

In that hour he himself would choose Nasetkin. She hesitated, yet could not keep from saying: and I, my father. Which, as he said, came to much the same thing.

Uller had all the continental contempt for the english. That his remarks might offend her never entered his mind. He never understood that she should care. Why should she? It was not a personal matter. It was simply german discipline and french logic united in contempt of a complacent and mentally lazy people.

They must have been amusing in england, he and Nasetkin, with their few selected canvases tied together with string with which to conquer London, having decided (finally) that Paris was hopeless unless one were an artist for wealthy prostitutes.

He told her about that as they walked back from Castola, the evening settling in uniform tepid blue and shadow. Women bearing heavy loads on their heads rustled past them in the dust like harmless grass snakes. Children with water-jugs slid by, singing with the shrill pointed voices of young cats. Cat-sound, cat-calling, which must surely have been the first human sound, anticipating speech? Now and again as though in answer to each other came a prolonged retching he-haw he-haw-haw-haw-haw . . . w . . . h-a-a-a-a-a-aq, dying in foolish and unprofitable lament. A parody of love, said Uller; a vocal satire on the culmination of passion.

At intervals along the cool shadow-gathering road they would walk into a wave of warm heavy air. It came grimly from under their feet. Reminding them, they agreed, after the manner of copy-book maxims or sermons in stone that All must Live as though About to Die, or that in the Midst of Life one is in Death, or that Although the Sun shines the Clouds are Gathering, and There is Always a Volcano underfoot. Which by some mental deviation she did not follow reminded him of england.

Needless to say they were back within a week. Nasetkin describing hilariously at the first glass and tearfully at the last how englishwomen wore thick flannel underwear, and never. Never. Was it believable? The barbarians. While he himself principally remembered that the rain was the wettest he had ever known, and that if one wanted a drink one went and stood up in a dark stale-smelling place where they sold nothing but port or whisky or a thick sticky beer which seemed brewed from putrid barley.

The main characteristic of the english, he considered, taking it all in all, was laughter. Chiefly at the expense of the foreigner. But on the whole at anything new or unusual. (From which she gathered that the few select canvases tied with string had not been handled with the respect due to them.)

He would even call laughter their national defence. It defended them against onslaughts of the mind. But fortunately for them the mistrusted foreigner did sometimes get past and beyond the defences, and, for their own good and after much resistance, showed them that there were other ways of using civilisation than drowning it in their tea-cups.

She must not think that he spoke idly or without giving full thought to the subject: but could she deny that it was these despised foreigners who had taught the english all that they knew? Did they not depend on the foreigner for the refinements of life as they depended for food? Allow no food-ships into england and in a month she would be physically starved. Allow no foreigner and she would be artistically starved. Until the foreigner came she had lived by bread alone. Were they not the one people in the world ignorant of what to eat, drink, or think? That this was true was proved by the fact that only those english who lived abroad or travelled much were fit to associate with. Once beyond the parochial confines of their narrow island space they became human (he thought) beyond recognition.

And what had the rest of the world to envy them except their capacity for believing any lie provided it was pleasant. Why? Because they were mentally lazy. That was why they mistrusted the french and mocked at the german thoroughness and love of knowledge as an end in itself. That was why they liked everything to be what they called: straightforward. No thinking; no knowledge of foreign languages; no desire to try and understand new problems and developments. It was so much easier and quicker to laugh. Which made other nations regard them as hypocrites. Untrue, unfair. It was merely a certain rustic straw-sucking simplicity in the midst of a complicated and exacting civilisation.

To the english a pictorial flower of civilisation is a hunting-field or a garden party, remarked Uller to the evening sky. And one must know everyone there. Whom one does not know one ignores. An englishman's greatest sin is not murder or rape or incest. Such vulgar passionate offences. No. It is wearing an incorrectly coloured tie with the wrong cut of coat; or having to admit that he is not a gentleman never having been to Eton; or that he has not sufficient money in his pocket to pay for his meal. That is as far as an englishman's soul's embarrassment can go.

On the continent (it seemed) a man looking at his fellow thinks: I am as good as you. In england a man looking at man thinks: thank god I am not as impossible as you. His pleasure is not in looking up but in looking down. A sly servile movement. The trait of a servant.

Not that he did not like the english. He was beyond racial prejudice of any kind. She must not think that because one understood a nation's faults one did not also recognise its virtues. Besides some of his best friends were englishmen. And he had told them what he thought of them as a whole every whit as freely as he spoke to her now.

—No doubt you astonished them.

—You cannot astonish an englishman, said Uller drily. You can only shock him.

H e made many sketches of her and finally painted her in her worn island clothes with Giovanni on her lap. Giovanni naked, pugnaciously naked and glowing like a goblet of heavy dark wine, the weight of the sun through thick leaves. She told him little or nothing about herself and as he preferred talking of himself he did not care sufficiently to press for confidences withheld. How he roared with laughter when told that in this case Hungerford was pronounced Hun'ard! But what, after all, when he had finished, did it matter? he asked. Creed, nationality, blood, how little they had to do with it all when one thought it out. That was what one could definitely admire about Christ: His getting beyond patriotism and nationality and preaching the brotherhood of man, which takes no account of colour, blood-tie, creed. The brotherhood of man: that was all He had meant in bidding them spread His message over the world. And that was, of course, the one part of His message they had taken such care not to spread!

The only possible brotherhood of man was the brotherhood of mind and trade. People with similar thoughts recognise each other the world over. The miner from Wales would recognise, understand, know instantly, the miner from North America, from Mexico, from Africa. The local grocer from a Berlin suburb is one with the local grocer from any white or coloured townlet. The architect only can grasp the problems of his fellow architect. The gambler—the gambler. The idle rich idles with his wealthy fellow. Those who speak the language of the brain or soul answer to that same brain or soul in another. Pick up any man, of any colour, of any creed, in any trade, in one corner of the earth and place him beside another man, of opposite colour and opposite creed, in the same trade at the other corner of the earth, and those two men will meet on the same ground: will know each other's problems: will be brothers: will talk together immediately in the language of work and common interest.

To Lisetta she had said that she would do her usual shopping and might then be going to Castellammare to see about that cart they had discussed. She might be away for a night or two. And might even spend some time at Sorrento. She was tired, of what precisely she could not say, but she had a sudden longing for change.

She went down to the beach with the rest of the household, watched him climb into Vincenzo's boat with the peasants and their parcels and melons and baskets of fruit, and be rowed out to the *Virgilio* blowing an apoplectic little whistle, advising them to be quick about it.

He was visiting Florence on the way home. He had said: I shall be back in Naples on the 18th. Had said where he would stay and at what hour he would arrive. They could go to Ravello; anywhere; Rome, Viterbo: he left her the choice. She would be there? That was all. Yes, she would be there because she liked his way of asking; of keeping it down to the level of the commonplace.

She took the midday boat. The *Virgilio* blew its apoplectic little whistle for her also, just as she was being handed up to the large man with the ropes, hanging his face like a harvest moon over the water, to see what more there was to come. Some-one was waving from the house. From far she watched Nicola, apish and alert, leaping about the hot sands, gathering in the red-brown fishing nets.

What to do with the few hours left to her? She was restless and undecided and must compose herself. She turned from the torrid seething streets whose noise usually delighted her to the cool of la villa. Through an opening in the heavily clustered trees she saw the idling carriages and the carts musical with bells and high silver trappings and scarlet tassels clattering along the white road bordering the intensely blue sea, towards the rocky outline of the Castel del Ovo.

She sat beneath the twisted uneasy olive trees watching a group of workmen working at a flower bed, and children playing in the sandy dust-white path. At intervals a child's scream filled the vaulted branches with echo. Now and again an older child picked up a younger one, held it tightly with passionate play against its breast, kissed its face again and again, and released it, struggling. Little boys were obstreperous. Little girls seemed to have vowed away their lives to the unbuttoning of their small brothers.

Later an elderly man joined her on the bench, staring in an uneasy way at her upheld profile. After a while with his stick he began tracing in the dust the outline of a shield with armorial bearings. He drew slowly, with care and flourish. She knew that it was meant for her. The ageing aristocrat-professor, reduced, deposed, unable to forget. All hanging out of the tops of their medieval towers, tapestry-wise, shaking fists at their neighbours. At one time (she remembered reading) there were three hundred of these towers with fist-shaking aristocrats leaning from their tops, in Lucca alone: but this was too much even for the insignia-loving italians, so they pulled down all but the twenty or so remaining today. And here was one of them, as it were, shaking his fist on the ground. She knew exactly what she would hear by showing an interest in his solemn dust scrapings. But today she was incurious and unconcerned. Besides, she felt that nothing he could tell her would be as interesting as the thing he did not tell. So after waiting, waiting, contemplating it in studied sadness, chin on stick, he made a quick impatient movement, thrust the toe and heel of his boot all over it, rose and walked away. He was offended; he made her feel as though she had struck a blow. She watched him walk stiffly, primly away in laborious search with the back of his head, with his very coat-tails, for another bench, another dusty design, a more discriminating spectator.

She sat on and on looking at what was happening around her; and then quite suddenly she too stood up and turned away. She walked quickly away from the bench towards the street. She did not want. She just did not want. Suddenly, she had no desire. She walked out of the gardens and hailed a carrozzella. There were exactly twenty minutes in which to get to the Cumana and catch the last boat from Baia. The carriage bumped noisily over the stones and she sat stiff-backed and purposeful, devoid of feeling. She did not want. Again it had been mental, as sensation came to her. And even had she missed passion in her life, which she had, now that it was offered her she did not want it.

Suddenly, like that; making her get up and leave the giardini and hurry to catch the last boat. Later in Foria it would be otherwise. In thought he would come to her again. Thinking, she might regret, often. She would not forget. He took place beside her father: part of her life. She did not feel that she would belong more to him by possessing him. She drew back from the thought of contact; half-willing, unable. Later, much later, she might understand why she had turned away so abruptly from the shouting children and the men at work over the flower bed. She would magnify it, worry it. A person, an episode, ridiculous, inconsequent, could remain with her rehearsed and reënacted for years. She could not help it, whose whole life had been but a struggle to accept and dismiss. And soon, when it was too late, perhaps because it was too late, she would be curiosity itself and regret, unnerved. And he would be real again and have some quality of the sun about him: the cold northern sun or a large white star. But just now sitting stiff-backed and devoid of feeling as the horse toiled up the steep Via di Toledo to her last train, he seemed not more than a large overpowering man, far too talkative and self-assertive and ill-mannered; and not a little heavy-fleshed for a lover. Yet she could not rid herself of the feeling that in betraying him she had betrayed herself. Yes, she had said she would be there.

Hearing the crowing of the ship's whistle she wanted nothing so much as to go out and weep; so irresolute she was, as a nun about to break her vows and unable to do so.

N ow Padre Antonio could return to the patting of childish heads and reassume the authority of his threadbare soutane. Maria need no longer tiptoe across the flat roof in jealous stealth, her hands loaded with pieces of rock to throw at her brothers dismissed from their sittings. She herself could return to the solitude from which she had been unwillingly roused. Now nothing could trouble her more. Lisetta had promised that no other guests would be accepted.

She was glad to settle back once more and see the clouds rise like swans unfurled from the heights of Vomero, catching the sun's last look and bearing it to her. It even seemed that, idling on the stairs and parapet, the two pigeons, white as the Holy Ghost, regained their innocence and once more entered an earthly paradise. (Leda, as he had said, was a woman too easily satisfied.) As he had said. As he had once remarked. At all moments of the day he said or he once remarked. Yet it was good to be alone again. Like a blade thrust in her in some drama of passion she grasped the handle of her solitude, pressing it to her with no regrets. It satisfied to tears. Sufficient as lines taken at random from Landor.

Long long ago she had felt it in her, when always the cliffs must be bare, the road reaching out to the edge of the moor, deserted; where her eye looked out over it all only her eye must look. Possessing only where none shared. Her view and her sky. By whose right? But there it was. A few trespassers on her road, a movement on her cliff, and she would turn away her eyes and feel like crying, small though she was, her arm hung up to his hand. He looked, too. Together they looked across at the Isle of Wight lying like a whale on the water, ready to sink slowly and without sound. Together they looked: the only person with whom she had looked as one.

Now once again she could walk on the earth alone. Walk by the sea alone. Walk to the Pineta, over the red stubble lit with shadow, umber stubble and pine needles and mounds of grey-black volcanic stone, and peeled mosaic of tree trunks; and sit on the ground under pines rising to intense silvery cloud-puffs bound together by red sinews; alone. It made her feel light and unreal and transparent, this belonging again to herself; of being one with the orchestration of scent and sound: blend of incense and manure: heaven and earth. As she looked back at the sky through the spread filigree of branches, she thought how Time, the sadist, held no terrors for her. That is given as compensation, it seems, to the lonely of heart. What happened to the earth, she felt, must happen to her seeing that there she would sit will-less and wait for it to happen.

Six years now. She hoped they had forgotten her; and doubted it. She thought with horror of living on in the thoughts of others. To be living on in thoughts which never rise to the surface of the face. Eyes and eyes letting nothing through and behind them those thoughts in which, against one's will, one was imprisoned. Even the escaping dead were not allowed their oblivion in these thoughts going on and on behind shuttered eyes. Embalmed in speechless eyes; thoughts endlessly spinning the shrouds of their dead; more contaminating than earthworms. She did not want to be contaminated by their thoughts. To escape she had brought her child away, that together they might be free of the thoughts of others. She did not want aspects of herself lying like a half-read letter on the floor of other people's minds. She hoped she was forgotten as the dead forget with grave-worms behind their eyes for thought.

So, to cheat herself, she assumed that she was forgotten. She too in time must forget everything that had been. In oblivion, she knew, lay freedom. Who chose to die must be allowed to die, though one's coat were being jerked off, and one leg was already half over the parapet.

H e wrote to her little more than a year later, at the end of November, 1914. What the mind took in of it and made its own would have to wait, she knew it looking down in a frown at the words as though willing them to regain their distinct outline and lie straight again across the page, for the worms to erase. *You who have wisdom but no peace. . . . my wife eager as other wives for the sacrifice. . . . excited by papa's brave uniform. . . .* How horrible it was, his letter! It was that shuddering sound which she still could not grow used to, of the bucket plunging down down down into the well and striking the water at last with a drowning cry as the heart, released, dropped in the breast. What had he to do with it all, this mean commercial débâcle? He could not fight. He could not kill. And at the thought he cried out to her. He abandoned himself as a child crying at the night. He held out his hands. *A vagabond, a stranger to you, wrapped in loneliness, sat down one winter's night to rest and cry a moment.*

For it seemed that he had missed her: had missed her as a sail misses the wind: a seed the soil: a shepherd boy a crown: a greek horse, wings.

W ar came to Foria in a few restrictions; from far a passing battle-ship; an airplane sighted. Later the women and boys replaced a few men in the vineyards and at the ports; and much more money was asked for the fruit and vegetables sent to the mainland. Now and then a search would be made of the house, the carabinieri, concluded and assertive, kicking open doors with the toes of their boots; so many were the students from the Naples schools evading service by taking refuge in the woods and vineyards.

Suspended in island space she watched it all, knowing she could do nothing with herself that would prevent or alleviate one drop of suffering or blood. It seemed a matter of hundreds of thousands of tons of high explosives against hundreds of thousands of men who had nothing whatsoever against each other, and were being ladled, thrown-in, fed into the slaughter with such a lip-service of brave-sounding finality as to turn the onlooker to stone: to something tearless and without sound, so cold, so premeditated, so inexorable was the hourly slaughter of men who had nothing whatsoever against each other. At first it did seem that at any moment something must happen; that some monstrous retribution was about to be visited on them. Any day now the earth must open, swallow, and have done with it. Or be rushed madly whirling through space to strike the throne of God itself and there crumble to a small grey dust such as is retrieved for urn burial after the ordeal by fire.

Why scramble to stick one finger more in the hell's broth? Already enough were treating it as a giant picnic: not a little dangerous but great fun, great fun. Awful it was to stand there weeping for the world, weeping for the folly of it all, for the foolish people, the foolish foolish people who were being ladled, rained into it in their hundreds of thousands, so that one could hear the grind and thud of the machinery as it caught, ripped up and threw away before one could warn them (standing there, looking toward the mainland; having no right at all to all these tears at the world's death). For no voice could pierce the thud-thudding of machinery. Enough. Stop. One moment only. O stop one moment only and think! And then when at last it had to stop, then tears were turned to laughter. For one had to laugh if one read carefully but not too seriously (for surely they were not meant to be taken too seriously?) the solemn nobly chosen words which were being hung about the brows of elderly born leaders of men by elderly born leaders of men (of those remaining of course) around oblong and horse-shoe shaped tables, among nobly hollowed inkwells and reverently struck pens, and prancing gilt pilastres and carved and ornamental mirrors: all in the very best period of a gypsy's vision of the Almighty's personal caravan.

How he went to the war she did not know. Official news was scarce. No english newspapers were to be had. But she felt it would be all very clean and smiling and neat and dutiful; and it was sad to think of things dark, such as blood and dirt and suffering, coming the way of one so clean and dutiful and believing in it all whole-heartedly; and capable of beautiful heroisms and sacrifices beyond human conception because of this unalterable cleanliness and belief. Not for him the sudden cry in the night, the sense of futility, the anger at being dressed up to aim death at one's fellow-men. For him the correct, the fortunate attitude which clothed him in an added armour of valour and strength. Lord! what then lies behind the eye of man that can so alter the perspective of his soul as to bring to one courage and decision and to the next anger and futility? A vagabond, a stranger to you, sat down one winter's night: and there he was somewhere on the mainland, loathing it, cursing it, being bitter and ineffectual to tears; and caught up and ladled in indifferently with all who died at peace knowing now a mother, a sister, one's growing children, wives, young women whose warmed faces smiled in breast pockets above Love and To My, a cottage, many acres, a room, whatever space theirs in which to place their own: protected. And there he was in a german uniform whereas if he had any pride in nationality at all, which was doubtful, it lay in the fact that for all his square bones and blondness he stressed the french blood in him, no matter to whom the strip Alsace-Lorraine belonged at the time of his arrival on it.

Like a watcher from another world she would stand and look across at the mainland, stopping short in her walk to realise, to try to grasp, that the sun shone over all, or rain fell, and the year went through its gestation, birth, and death, and nothing was changed, not one single leaf its colour or wave its way in response to the monstrous happenings across a small strip of water. The earth cared not at all. Then the mechanism of its changes became awful to her. No more was she impressed by the grand manner of the sun working its will on the earth. Purpose and dignity (so childish she became, standing there, feeling how terribly it all mattered) seemed to have left it; remained a slow blindfolded mule moving endlessly round and round and round the waterwheel, stubborn, undeviating, fettered. The earth then was not for man, but man (what a harvest he was garnering now!) was for the earth. The earth caring not at all.

Nor for that matter, she thought, roused by the sudden sound of footsteps, did Padre Antonio, ascending in priestly leisure the path to the cemetery and engrossed in his breviary as though it were the very latest news.

A ll of which was long ago. So long ago, she thought, settling the cushions more comfortably behind her head, that she had become a legend in some sort, and a group of tourists had recently come to stare openly at her, and now and then (did she turn suddenly aside in the street from a stall or a window) she would surprise whispers in her direction and nodding heads: so strange it was for a woman living on day after day and year after year and unable, if questioned suddenly, to find a reason. I never see a greek statue, he once said, without being grateful to Time for knocking off its head and arms. That was it. A statue without a head. Or was she not rather a head without a statue? A head, she decided, going back many years and remembering, a head without its statue.

Brave and serious her head; a little severe perhaps, judged by certain standards, but with a definite calm speechlessness of stone about it. A head, as he looked up suddenly at her unseeing upheld profile against the sky, that would sit well on the Victory of Samothrace: though he anathematised greek art and Michelangelo (pollution of the world, that man) there being no one, no one but his god Orcagna; and of course Pieter Breughel the elder; and a man whose name she could not remember who was, or had been, a clerk in a bank, or a customs official, and whom he had known in Paris; showing her most curious pictures of his work: one especially, a tiger leaping at an arab on horse-back (was that it?) in a jungle undergrowth cut in sabre-strokes, and telling her contemptuously (for she *could* not see) that it was one of the few pictures in the world that mattered. Though he loathed greek sculptural art, swearing by his egyptians and chinese, still her head (seen at this moment) would sit well on the Victory of Samothrace, the only one of them he could stand, who was in his bones in a sense. The Louvre's fault: the stupendous stage management of her, as one advances toward her hardly daring to place one foot before the other (with tears in the eyes for one is sixteen and has left home for this) coming to meet one on brave uplifted wings. And though later one loathed them all, their dianas and crouching venuses and soft-bellied youths, She remained: the headless woman. And later how right it seemed: there to accept man not to question him and complicate a simple and necessary act. Off, off with their heads! That was what men felt in their bones; the perfect, the headless woman. And there wor-shipped. Like that should she come to meet one on brave wings out-spread: but headless, headless. He was amazed at how well her head (at this moment, at this angle, angles and moments having much to do with the conduct of emotions) would fit: so brave and sightless it looked upheld on its neck-column.

Of which she was to know nothing for that was the morning Teresa Fusco's husband was drowned and he had behaved so disgracefully—

with such a deliberate childish rudeness—that she became speechless
and withdrawn with dislike of him. He had so clearly no intention of
leaving the widow to the enjoyment of her hour. One and a half litres
of strong wine Michele Fusco drank before going in the water and had
dropped like a stone. Yet why? He was a strong sixty-four and had
drunk his litre and a half before going in the water for the last fifty
years. Yet this morning in he went and dropped like a stone before the
children could reach him. That was at ten o'clock. By eleven Teresa
was already at the beach. Carved in some dark and ancient wood, her
island clothes wrapped tightly round her body and head, she sat on the
last step of the terrazza, rocking to and fro. A bodyguard of women
closed her in; a few children stood staring near their mothers. The
widow moaned and rocked herself. She wanted to take him home, she
cried. She wanted to take him home. But she must not, they murmured,
the doctor must see him first. The dead man lay covered by a sheet.
Why did the doctor not come? She wanted to take him home, she
moaned, rocking her thin body, holding it in her arms and swaying.
Now and again the women bent slightly forward and moaned with her.
They drew out the sound, seemingly spinning their grief. Feeling her
sorrow truly shared, the widow would make short sharp cries. Aia, she
cried. Aia, aia, aia, aia, aia, which was the pattern pricked out in relief.
Still, her eyes remained dry. How could water, she left one wondering,
ooze from something so dark-dried and withered? I want to take him
home, she said. And just then Uller began chasing Antonio in and out of
the tables. Immediately the centre shifted from the mourners to the
man laughing with the child. It was altogether a disgraceful performance. No, no, said his laughter, not so much fun for widows, if I can
prevent it; and he set about it with a vengeance. He knew, his attitude
proclaimed, that she was enjoying herself. Nasty old charlatan. Very
well, he sided with the husband. Soon it became a mimic and foolish
battle between husband and wife. He took the initiative by making a
louder noise. He knocked over a chair and shooed the cats back into the
house, and tickled Antonio till the boy rolled on the floor yelling and
kicking. You had better take a photograph of them, he shouted at her,
or shall I paint them for you? he is doing this for me, she told herself,
trying not to show how angry she felt. He is nothing but an obstreperous
child prancing before its mother. For it angered him most to see her
standing there taking it all seriously. A few tears, a moan, some-one
dead: and there you had it, the imbecile sisterhood of women. What
they called sympathy: and immediately it flowed from them this pity,

like. Yes, like that. How impatient, how unclean women made one feel with their communal ready sympathy and will-to-weep.

Below, the widow was trying to recapture the attention of her body-guard by louder groans and longer cries, but it was difficult to pierce the clatter of overturned chairs and rushing feet and of Antonio's suppressed giggles, for he had been told from the house to stop his noise. So she ceased moaning and sat taut and silent staring at the sea. The women refused to look up so angry they were, resenting it more than the death itself.

For my sake, she said to him finally, the noise having become something of an anti-climax, knowing how their anger included her. These people . . . (she looked down at the women's averted, closed faces: no, she could not say love or like or want) . . . these people respect me. He pretended to take no notice, but shortly afterwards he went indoors. Below they knew (and she knew that they knew) that she had asked him to be quiet and he had gone indoors and would make no more noise. The widow knew it instantly. It was absurd the way even the back of her head knew that the noise had ceased. Still, she waited before reassuming her sorrow. She waited perhaps six minutes. Then she began again. I want to take him home, she moaned. The tension relaxed, her bodyguard bent toward her once again. Aia, aia, she cried. Aia.

He was wrong to disturb them, she thought, if only artistically. For the mourning group, fitted there at the foot of the stairs, had an extraordinary Pietà rhythm. It assumed that sorrow-laden and tortured unity of a Crivelli Deposition. Mary, dried and withered under fierce suns, and her women (she felt) must have mourned Christ with much the same sounds and attitudes. It gave the whole a strangely impressive significance. The dead man could not have asked a more solemn keening. What does it matter, she felt, whether the widow is serious or not?

A carabiniere arrived; stood talking at a distance and nodding his head. They pointed the widow out to him: she was fixing him from far with her birdlike eyes. I want to take him home, she wailed to him. They told him what she had said. He shrugged his shoulders. Some-one brought out a chair and he sat down under the awning near the corpse, staring at the sheet. By now the women were growing so angry and impatient that several were in real tears. Where was the doctor? people were asking. What right had he to take two hours to drive from Castoli when it could be walked in twenty minutes?

At last well past noon the enormous black-bearded corsair of a doctor arrived; took no notice at all of what was said to him; took out a note-book, wrote in it, threw back the sheet, bent over the body, tapped, untied the bathing drawers: was quite useless but impressive. Against the white sheet the dead man lay like a mummy, as dark and as dried, his cheeks sucked in the hole of his mouth. The carabiniere, now less important, rose and said they could take the man away. Wound in the sheet they lifted him on the stretcher and carried him across the sands; the widow walking directly behind with bent head and holding a darkly angular hand across her face.

S ix o'clock. Curious the power of these bells to soothe or irritate. Either they set up a prolonged and angry farmyard cackling, or imitated the useless screech and crow of the women at the fountains for their turn, or cried out like lost and frightened children, or pealed with mock joy as for an old man's wedding. This evening San Soccorso shook out the hour in motes of sound incredibly pure and cold. I must remember Graziella's coat on Thursday, she thought.

It was a pleasant clear-eyed October (eager restless month which she preferred to them all) but already the sun was colder and the winds treacherous. Graziella, she reflected, must be protected against them. But must she? Why protected? And against what? Did it matter to any-one but herself (come, admit) whether Graziella were dressed in furs or packing-paper? Was she not, with that inborn climatic sentimentality which causes old ladies to leave their fortunes for the upkeep of free-born cats and undesirable dogs, making another mystery of the commonplace? Admit that the girl herself attached neither mental nor physical importance to the thing. Graziella was suddenly and instinctively proud of herself: and proud of the envy her swelling out-thrust body caused among the women as she passed, her head set well back, and with something of her mother's slow Ionic smile on her mouth. As thanks offering to the many-breasted Diana, twin-horns of the new moon, she wanted her silver offering. Which was to be the first of many: the Madonna would see to that! Nothing more.

Nothing of that mystic entrailless joy, that frail byzantinian hand-crossed expectation which culminated and died in Fra Angelico's cell, to be reborn again of Raphael as a comely rounded wench filled full with milk and sap. (Women in eastern art, as he had said, serving to suggest the unapproachable: in western art to remind one of one's mistress.) The woman's saint, this vacant-looking woman modelled to Raphael's taste with the plump child on her arm, above the light burning in every home, in every shop, on every street corner. How tired one grew of the tyranny of her placid mammiferous charm! Nothing here to turn maternity into a folly or a martyrdom (except those Seven Swords because her son did not want her). What have I to do with thee? he asked. And is punished by remaining ever helpless and small and plump in her strong maternal embrace: woman worshipped. (Had ever man in the grimmest stories of mythology, pondered Ruth, a more difficult punishment to bear?) Occasionally doubts pierced her woman's heart with Seven Swords, leaving her ennobled and more comely and acceptable than ever.

She had to admit that it was altogether ridiculous of her to sit worrying (with a ladylike mystic sentimentality) as to whether the girl was hot or cold whichever way the wind blew, or dropped her child behind a hedge or in a bed; when the girl herself was as indifferent to it all as God Himself breathing on His handful of earth and waiting (probably with His eyes shut) to see what He would bring Himself.

She thought of Lisetta's slow Ionic smile: that slow secretive smile lifting the edges of the lips and troubling the eyes an instant. It rarely came now: she had a kindly open laugh: but Ruth had surprised it on her many a time when she was young. Now in certain moments her daughter had it. It was unconscious, of course: and brief. Therein lay its arresting quality of wonder: (for could anyone, considered Ruth, be more empty-headed than Graziella?) And children, very young children, have it: and therein lies *their* charm. It comes before speech in some whole and mysterious way: infusing them with sudden reality and beauty as they lie staring at space. Which was why it was so beautiful to watch an infant smile. Smiling without words or spoken humour; with no need for a cultivated taste in buffoonery or the ridiculous. How far away one was from it all! Used up and old beyond recall one felt before the sight of a child making its own joy because of a texture, a soft hand, a silky sleeve, a sound, a colour. But with the coming of speech they lost it; as though by an added faculty of expression they weakened that of sensation: and nothing was left to wonder at but the commonplace.

Concetta certainly was without it. A fine large girl cut all in one, as it were, from a block of dark-coloured stone: the whites of her eyes and teeth all that had escaped the sun when it burnt her up in its prolonged splendour. For her mother Concetta worked as hard as a grown man; she swam like a fish; she was more devout than any novice. She prayed with pleasure and attended every Mass. From the age of ten she had been burning candles and wearing out her knees to Santa Restituta to help her to get to a favourite uncle and aunt in South America and work there: work hard and send money home like her brothers, and not miss, as she herself put it, all that was happening "outside."

She would bring Graziella's coat next Thursday (though admitting all the arguments against it!) and finish Concetta's jersey by tomorrow evening. She frowned thinking how she could have got the wool more quickly by going to the town for it herself; and with a presentiment that Graziella would come back empty-handed pretending that it had been impossible to find.

But she was to forget all about the red woolen jersey because before Graziella could get back from the town the letter came from Strathwick, Strathwick and Strathwick, & Goode, informing her that as her husband had made no alteration to his first will beyond a few recent personal bequests, they would be glad to have her instructions regarding the property and desired to assure her of their loyal and continued services in her interests, and coöperation in whatever plans she should decide on.

I must go back, she thought immediately. I must go back. She felt like a lady in a ballad. My husband is dead, is dead. And I must hame, must hame. Surprised: but more because it seemed unusually real than because it was unexpected. She was surprised and excited in a calm unreal way. It was as though waking from a long trance she had crossed the room and looked in the mirror and the mirror lay in bits and she must float away down the stream on a boat and the spell was broken. Was she glad? She could not be sure. Yet she felt that she had been waiting for this summons to return.

She decided on the four-o'clock boat for Naples, catching the seven something for Rome, changing immediately for Milan. And before going went to say good-bye to him. She found him lying asleep on the sand in the shadow of a rock where the children had left him.

To the end of life, it seems, one may find oneself looking at familiar things for the first time. Asleep and dressed and in the sunlight, and perhaps because she was leaving him and was to be free of him for the first time, she found him unusually interesting to look at with his fine thin nostrils and well-shaped mouth and the long silky eyelashes of an attractive woman. His shirt was open and the fairish brown hair on his breasts caught lights from the sun and shone like coarse silk. His bare throat was brown as were his hands, long thin-fingered hands like hers:

not a man's hands at all, she thought, contracting her brows. He held no menace for her. Dead he might look as he looked now. But should he open his eyes he might smile and speak to her, and jump up and insist on seeing her to the boat. (O why did you tell Polyphemus your *name?* I've been so anxious about you!) Is it possible, she thought walking away, that he will not know that I am gone? For that matter had he ever known that she was there? Whole he looked lying there in the shadow of the rock: whole and good to look on. How well he looked! Who, seeing him asleep, could believe? At that moment and for the first time it occurred to her how proud a woman she might have been. But he was rootless, null, unproductive: therefore not a living being at all. And all of her contriving. To punish her he would not know that she was gone.

Lisetta kissed her hand: there were tears in her eyes.

Night fell quickly and blotted out the vines and farmsteads and mulberry garlands holding hands from tree to tree, as the train sped toward Rome. Moon and stars were very bright and purposeful. The bold dark outline of the hills against the pale intense moonlight gave an eerie impression of a cavern opened suddenly under the sky. As though, as she sat there looking from the window, the bottom had dropped out of the heavens.

S he woke and looked out on Tuscany. It was early: barely five o'clock.

The light alone was as nothing she had ever seen or imagined. Calm, limpid, and emptied of all colour. The grey-blue olive trees broke from the Tuscan earth in ghostly waterfalls. The very cypresses pointed their fingers gently as from a Holy Hand. She recalled his contemptuous dismissal of Tuscany: one is perpetually attending a Last Supper.

Yes, it was like that. The umber rising of the hills moulded with how gentle a thumb, and then smoothed by angels with mystic tender feet. No Titan ever strode across them or lay imprisoned beneath. Their very outlines were caressed. What an infinity of patience had gone to the making of this land, she marvelled. On the summit of each small hill a modest-gazing castle. Gentle campanili; a narrow silvered river; long dressed fields; and sorrowing cypresses in slow procession up the gently moulded hills. Infinitesimal cities sown on hillocks; the houses in their varnish of centuries so neatly fitted in the hollows; so eager; so stippled with brightness. And never an angry look. Sweet-sweet as a thrush song at dawn.

She remembered Uller's remark: baroque is a man who talks too loud and too long. And thought of the palatial arrogance of Naples. Its high-cast ceilings; its monstrous doorways breathing defiance; its colossal façades of tossed-up and floating stone. And with it went the ferocious southerner, round-shouldered, bull-necked. Even the southern houses, she reflected, had large mouths.

No trace here of the bravado of baroque. And all at once she knew what gave that look of warmth and friendliness. She must have known it at once. Once again she saw houses with roofs! Home! Roof—synonym of home. Friendly as thatch; as those brown-sagging roofs hung like fishing-nets over old and much-lived-in cottages. She must, she thought again, have known it at once. How long ago now since she had seen a roof? How far, how very far away it was from the sun-baked flat-roofed house which had become more real to her than her childhood's home.

The ascetic land: the land of Saint Francis, silver-green, even-coloured, cool. Its churches modest, its outline meek and smiling. Yet the earth's blood (she thought) is hot blood, is rich dark volcanic blood. No no. Frail and lovely though it was she was glad she had not stopped there on that adventurous journey south of long ago. She would not have found peace here, she felt, where peace was so orderly and even-breathed. Here in Tuscany all was beatific calm. Foria wild and disorderly was for ever drawing breath between one rage and another. No, no. After the first eye-filling wonder she regained her balance. Here I would have grown meek, she thought, resisting the spell. The limpid morning breeze would have condoned with her. The stippled green surface was too much of a caress. Rest on me it seemed to say. I bear all burdens. And in the end she would have emerged splendidly wronged and purified. No; Tuscany was best left to elderly water-colour enthusiasts, and to those incredible englishwomen abroad in gaunt raffia-trimmed hats and with large coloured beads around their necks, who look always an uncared-for thirty-seven.

When the train drew into Florence at something past six she could not resist the temptation. It would delay her: but who expected her? Who was there to expect her or know that she was coming? She had only herself to answer to. She could catch an afternoon train and leave Milan at midnight.

She was glad that she saw it first empty save for the people themselves: carters, peasants, cleaners, workers on their way to work. Even so, and at its best, she was disappointed. It was neither one thing nor the other. Time was scattered about it in such disharmony as to make it neither past nor present. And it was definitely a woman city. Its face that of a woman smiling a sad and painted smile. Ineffectual and womanly, she thought, as its history: the not very serious warfare: the not very formidable priests: the pageantry of elegance and Madonna-worship: the respectability of its honest tradesmen and artist-craftsmen. Florence was ever the bourgeois of italian cities!

Once I should have loved all this, she thought, coming out on the Cathedral square unexpectedly. She felt cheated. She blamed Browning. For instance, his Giotto. Coloured sugar stick, she thought: and the Duomo. Coloured sugar stick, she thought again, resenting it, hurrying past the clanging trams. Were they never to be serious? For instance, that unruly heap of statuary in the Loggia which even her eye could see as irritating as it was out of place. And was that the David? He was right, she thought, who a moment since would no more have dared question Michelangelo than a child dares question god. That white giant, far far too white (she thought) against the dark grim-proportioned Signoria (a welcome male touch: the first so far) with his soft woman's belly and pensive face? Soft-bellied and white he stood like a naked woman in the serious setting of walls and cobbles dipped in the mellow dye of centuries. He had no business there. She knew it though seeing him for the first time, and yet for hundreds of years he had been allowed to stand without protest and cripple the beauty of the setting. But the Signoria was gorgeously serious. Good, too, the Palazzo Strozzi, and strong and angry-looking. How well a frown sits on a house, she thought, pleased. And now and then on suddenly turning aside one did come upon a mass of stone heavy and male and not built to house women-saints and courtesans.

Already by eight o'clock the congestion and noise so typical of Florence and more irritating and nerve-wrecking than anywhere else in Italy, were making themselves felt; and even the narrowest streets were alive with the coachmen's wild whip-cracking and bicycle-riders bearing down on pedestrians who took refuge in divine providence and sublime indifference. Escaping into the Piazza Santa Croce where Time has been least tampered with, she was doubly delighted because of its unexpectedness. And standing on the Ponte Vecchio looking now this way now that she admitted its charm, and leaned on the railings thinking that, after certain angles of Paris, this was probably the most familiar view in the world.

For the first time, leaning there, she heard english spoken. She picked them out from far: tweeds, mackintoshes over arm though the sky was radiant, coloured beads, long self-conscious strides and that look of cultivated indifference assumed by those english-speaking abroad to show the onlooker (always the onlooker, she thought) that this was neither new nor to be wondered at. It's a *great* mistake. Never tell them. Never say. So I said. Most comfortable, most, and only. Yes, I know. Yes. I know. Like it? No'bad. Ha. Ha ha ha. A'right. So I said. Never pay. My dear, do *you? Do* you? Yes. Ha ha. O yes. 'Right. Ha. O no O *no.* When an Italian says *that,* dear, it means.

Having been walked over the view was now somewhat bedraggled, as is the way with certain views and certain people. At a sound it had become a suburb of heaven. There was a voice that breath'd o'er Eden touch about it. A celestial garden city. We are full to capacity at the moment, she heard Saint Peter saying, looking up from the register and being helpful. Until the alterations are complete would you care to go to Florence? Charming spot. In a sense quite as pleasant. The same people and all that. And the views quite quite charming. You will like it there I feel sure.

The stern frown of the Pitti palace restored the balance. What character a house with a menace in it has, she thought, retracing her steps over the Ponte Vecchio and stopping to stare in a window of Art reproductions and Views. And there, to the side of the window, leaning against the reproduction in colour of a fresco-fragment by Nardo di Cione, a picture somehow familiar. I know that picture, she thought. And then stared again and lost thought of where or why she stood there. Giovanni stared back at her from stark blue-black eyes set in an incredibly blue face against an incredibly blue sky. She read Moderner Meister der Farbe. Das blaue Kind. The blue boy. Le garçonnet bleu. Vom elsässischen Maler: Hans Uller, 1884-1916.

So it was in the Tate Gallery. She would go there. Some-one then, something was there to meet her in London. It was a friendly thought. There must be other things of his. There must be books and reproductions. But these she would reserve: she would wait. She turned away from the window and into the maze of narrow streets, following where they led. What had guided her to Florence? Suppose she had not stopped: had reached Milan and not known, perhaps never known, that though Uller was dead Giovanni stared from the walls of a great gallery and made London no longer strange to her. They turned to stare at the tall brown-faced woman striding along smiling at the pavement.

She heard him say: genius is sanity. Genius is only sanity. Genius is common sense uncommonly used. Pick out the men of genius in the world and you have picked out the few sane men. Throw in certain grades and degrees of talent and men who excel at certain jobs. When the rest of mankind comes to die the only thing you can be sure of is that while they lived they helped fill the sewers. That was why, he said, the world's experience was always wasted and why the world repeated its mistakes. Only two people had ever profited from the lessons of the past: the artist and the scientist. The one understood beauty: the other truth.

And from that, apropos of nothing, he must tell her of Nasetkin's taste in women. He had to have them respectable and married. They were cleaner, he said. (Frenchwomen are best but not over-clean.) Wives of local mayors and minor deputies and officials, not too easy to get but once got most willing and yet needing none of the difficult wooing of unskilled virgins. Also, being a russian, Nasetkin liked to think that he brought pleasure into the lives of married women. Then would come such amorous incidents which he found so amusing as hardly to be able to begin for laughter, such as Nasetkin's wooing of the wife of the Maire of the . . . arrondissement, an enormous eighteen-stone creature fit for a circus tent; and how feeling that some heroic and decisive gesture was needed Nasetkin decided to lift her up and carry her to the divan in his manly arms and bumped and staggered about the room dragging the back part of her about the floor in a terrifying effort to lift her up, crashing into furniture edges and bouncing back and not daring to drop her for fear the divan wasn't there. All he knew was that every time she gave a shriek he had impaled some corner of her on the furniture. Until at last she found sufficient breath to hiss at him: no, it was not repeatable. And Nasetkin hurt and indignant panted back: and that also was not repeatable. At the time she had not thought it amusing, so shocked she was at the thought of anyone repeating such a story to her, and knowing that he repeated it only to shock her, miming with huge delight through the absurd comedy. He rocked, he roared with laughter! The englishwoman's fear of being treated as a woman!

Yet here she was laughing at the memory of it as she strode with amazon stride through the streets of the celestial suburb not caring where she went and walking straight into the mercato centrale filled with rich sounds of tuscan peasants calling attention to their wares, to the profusion of flat plaited baskets heavy with autumn fruits and leaves and making it a thing of sound and colour to hold the breath at.

Fruit and peasants again: how right they were! How purposeful and serious they looked. How unalterable it all was. And what a good smell it had, as she stood breathing it all in, full of gratitude to them and thinking how they, the people, had saved their city.

Leaving it she came into a piazzetta of no distinction but quiet and tree-bordered and with stone slabs of benches at intervals under the trees. She sat down. The morning had excited her, revived her, brought life back slowly in her veins. She had not felt the life around her so deeply for years, nor felt so free from care. She knew now that he was dead. She had always known it: but now she knew the year in which he died. Nearly fourteen years ago, and it was as yesterday! How the years had passed without her noticing them, as she sat there with the very best butter in her watch at an unreal ceaseless tea party with Richard and her father and Hans the unreal ceaseless guests. All at once it had become fourteen years and an eternity of time. Before she had known the date it was but yesterday. But it was all long ago.

She heard a cry and saw a small child of three standing between a quiet-looking tall woman and a man in working clothes. The woman was trying to distract the child's attention so that the man might reach his bicycle at the side of the road and ride away. They made a little game: the child followed it for a moment but always as the man reached his bicycle she turned and with a cry rushed at him. So he had to return and pretend that he did not want to go. He held the child in his arms and she clung to him and held on to his neck with her little hands. Then he put her down and again the cry was wrung from her. Ruth watched her contorted face and pitied her. All the passions were set on it. All jealousy, all despair was on the small contorted face and in the cry she gave. Finally the woman lifted her in her arms; and the man gave her a last kiss and ran to his machine and was off waving to her till he turned the corner. She struggled; she cried; she beat her little hands. Not more than three, thought Ruth. Passionate, despairing little thing! What would become of her, she wondered? What mistakes would she make?

The woman stood unperturbed smiling at the child's distress and stroking her soft tassels of honey-coloured hair.

—Was that her father? asked Ruth.

—No, said the mother. His wife nursed her while I was in hospital for nearly two years. He comes here to see her sometimes.

The woman took the child away to the other end of the square. The little creature came no higher than the stone benches, and now and then

Ruth would see a little head rise over a bench, still looking in the direction of the man who had fled on his bicycle.

She took a carrozza and drove to San Marco.

The office boy gave it as his opinion that Mr Benjamin Strathwick was not tin. But he would go and make sure. No, Mr Benjamin was sow, but Mr Nathaniel was sin. Sin but engaged. Could she wait?

He was a nice small boy, quite clean. After handing her an evening paper he went back to the licking of stamps in a dark corner. She left the newspaper on her knees and sat staring into the tired-looking face. You'll 'ave to wait a long time for Mr Nathaniel, he called to her, they always 'as.

So (not to hurt the office boy's feelings) she opened the paper and found herself reading a ladylike tea-pale eulogy of foreign travel: the peculiar charm of Venice. After which she read an interview with a bishop headed: I believe in a Heaven for Dogs. After which she read an article in which a Dean was tolerant and clear-minded on Religious Intolerance. A small square was drawn on the page in which one read that the views herein expressed were brilliant, were startling, and would shed new light on a parlous subject and the editor took no responsibility. (From which she gathered that the value of being a clergyman in modern journalism was that one could write pale essays acceptable to the average man of moderate newspaper culture and win renown as a reactionary.) She was about to learn the moral the Bishop of London drew from the declining birthrate when a bell rang and the office boy wanted to be followed this way, please, and she was shaking hands with some-one thin and grey and incredibly tall, and then sitting down in a dusty and traditional leather chair in the dusty and traditional legal setting.

Just as one may come suddenly on one of those reed-voiced thin-necked curates who cannot be bettered, so outwardly Mr Nathaniel Strathwick was all that a solicitor of repute and long-standing should be, to the very finger tips upholding finger tips. With how dry a smile he uttered cold and amiable words of no consequence. With what precision of look and utterance he gave polite and meaningless remarks the authority of a legal decision. Three weeks? Ah, then she could no longer be considered a stranger, Mrs Rice-Hungerford. He used return and once more in England with such finality that she hastened to assure him that she had come only for as short a stay as possible and was returning almost at once. As soon, it seemed, as the business on which she had come was settled. (Why, she wondered, should a human being spread his fingers wide as a cat stretches a paw, and dance on their tips?) Aah. It was both a sigh and a question. For a fraction of a second Mr Nathaniel Strathwick sought to remember and allowed it to be seen that he sought to remember. Exactly. The something queer, the something, exactly, about the young person his late client had married, let me see, how many years would that be exactly?, against the family wishes. Returning almost immediately? (Could it be that Mr Nathaniel Strathwick was disappointed and displeased?)

And Sharvells? It seemed that after giving it much thought (which was why she had postponed her visit until now) Sharvells was to become the permanent home of a charitable institute which provided holidays for London's slum children. Though the scheme was really more comprehensive than that. It was to be a permanent all-the-year round home for poor children who were weak or had been ill, and especially for ill-treated children; at certain times of the year (they were hoping to arrange) slum mothers could take their holidays with their children. It had nothing to do with mentally defective children, she hastened to explain, who were in no sense, she believed, worth saving.

London on reacquaintance appeared a vast children's hospital. She was appalled. (Now he has ceased dancing on his finger tips, she thought.) For Mr Nathaniel Strathwick was quite overcome. He admitted as much. It was the last thing, he said, that he had expected to hear. A sudden spark of pity struck in him for his late client who against the family wishes had once married this eccentric woman sitting opposite him, staring him in the face with steady eyes. (Hard, thought Mr Strathwick. Determined sort of woman. Difficult type of woman to deal with. Not what one could call a womanly woman, thought Mr Strathwick who was usually most careful to get in first with any staring to be done.) He used words such as heirloom and family (who *was* she exactly? he cast about in his mind) and pride, and to his listener's astonishment, touched on the matter of tradition and gave a short apologetic résumé of dates and then stopped suddenly (would the woman never take her eyes off his face?) and said that before this thing, before any irrevocable step was taken, had she thought of selling Sharvells? He spoke of commendable impulse, of the generosity responsible for such a (proposed) gift. But in these hard days of taxation it was not a wise or light undertaking to throw away, he stressed the words throw away, both profit and property. (Again she noticed how an over-bred english voice can be a thing detached from the speaker: not rising warm and articulate from the lungs or even from the pit of the stomach, but emerging clipped and thin from the oval of the palate.) She caught the words hotel and golf-course. It seemed that the country had great need of golf-courses easy of access at week-ends. From no point of view (having always the interests of his clients at heart) could he assure her that the course she proposed taking was practicable. Such a scheme, he said, would involve a very great deal of money: a considerable part of which, he said, had already been swallowed in death duties.

There were the pictures, she said. She had been told, and had sought information for herself, that Gainsboroughs and Constables and the English School reached high prices just now. They could all go. Then there was the furniture. Most of the land beyond the woods could be sold. The tenants would be only too pleased to buy their own land. Whatever money coming to her under the will would remain as a yearly income for the running expenses (she had it seemed her own money which more than sufficed); the money from the sales could go to the necessary alterations to the place. It would not be expensive to run as the children would do practically all the work (under a new training scheme) their own gardening, producing their own food. The great thing was that the Society should have a home and headquarters and an income of its own, so as not to be entirely dependent on a precarious and reluctant charity.

But, said Mr Nathaniel Strathwick. But, said the intently staring woman, the spirit in which it was given mattered even more than the gift. The thing must be believed in by everyone. Most of all by those who drew up deeds and saw to contracts. She knew nothing of such things, but it was a work she believed in: had set her heart on. She had found that those with whom she had discussed and planned it, certain heads of the Society, those who were to be responsible for its running, were glad of it, were sure of its success: were enthusiasts. One did not want the legal advisers of a holiday home for poor children to sulk (nothing Uller ever said to Padre Antonio pierced so deeply as that unseemingly-used word of an eccentric woman pierced the senior partner of Strathwick, Strathwick and Strathwick, & Goode) to sulk because it was not an exclusive hotel or golf club. In such work people must be eager, said the eccentric woman as though she were referring to a sporting contest or a dancing troupe. They must be enthusiasts.

(Young people, she thought, watching his cold grey face controlled by some inner self-willed mechanism rather than by blood and muscle, with young alive teeth to smile down at them and young alive voices and with young healthy-looking flesh on their arms and cheeks.) He counselled her so strongly against it would it not be wiser for him to drop the matter and for her to go, she hesitated, perhaps to the Society's own? On which immediately Mr Nathaniel Strathwick smiled the disarming and helpless smile of one who has been in the wrong and is suddenly convinced of it and generously admits his error; and the scheme became laudable and of an assured success and an enterprise with which one might well be proud to be associated.

I n the sky a moon: round, solid, luminous. She crossed King's Bench Walk making for the Embankment. The evening was cold but unusually clear. Enormous coloured electric signs continually effacing themselves and trying again were powerless to detract from the beauty of the hurrying swollen river. On the South Side, thrust in irregular outline against the sky, massive blocks of dark warehouse walls lit suddenly by the glare of light, assumed the weird shape and colour of those burning backgrounds on which, in old pictures, Lot's wife looks back. She would walk, she decided, as far as Waterloo Bridge, to where Big Ben stared like a surprised and haughty owl. Weeks of sooty rain and dreary wetness made a walk an event to her.

She was growing used to London, but not reconciled. It still grated on her sense of beauty and fitness like an ill-timed laugh. She was still unable to believe the noise, the lack of air, the crowded come and go of roads and pavements. The shabby down-at-heel greyness everywhere surprised and dismayed her. Where then was that sense of spaciousness, of quiet beauty, of arched necks taut on their bearing reins, of green trees, of great squares more solemn than a cathedral close, which had remained with her through the years from her rare visits after her marriage. It was not so much the noise. She was used to noise. Nothing could be more noisy than Naples. (If it came to comparisons then the eight or ten women haggling over their wares in the piazzetta at Foria Ponte could reduce the most tumultuous London street to a whisper!) But there is such a thing as harmonious noise, integral part of sun and sky, and there is a grey monotonous clamour under torn and hesitating skies, hanging down over all like an old beggar woman's unkempt hair.

A vast children's hospital, she had said to that incredibly tall and leathery man who had stared at her from small restricted grey-blue eyes, hesitating whether to treat her as a lady or a lunatic for wishing to deprive the empire of a golf-course within easy reach. Is it useless? Will it help in any way? she wondered.

A tramcar hurtled past like a rocket. In depression sudden noise has an angry and menacing sound. She started as though, tearing past, some-one had screamed at her. Was the gift of Sharvells merely the gratification of an ill-considered and quixotic impulse? At most six hundred children at a time: from how many hundreds of thousands? And was it fair to lift them out of it for a week or month and throw them back again? Could she take that responsibility? And did it matter whether a few people more or less ate or did not eat, breathed or did not breathe? Doubt left her suddenly bitter and discouraged.

Had it always been like this? Which of us has altered, she wondered, coming on it with new and startled eyes: at its winter's worst, perhaps. She had no right (and no need) to notice such things having been driven straight to the discreet and exclusive hotel in Hans Crescent where people coming from the country looked neither grey-faced nor under-fed, and where one did not have to walk quickly, consciously using as little breath as possible, through narrow foetid streets, as though the promiscuous herded millions in their interminable ribbons of dirty street had emptied themselves on the air and the passer-by must lunge through it as best he can. But she could not help seeing what was there to be seen, nor moving beyond that airy strip between Piccadilly and the few discreet squares of Kensington and Belgravia where the view was less drab and time-tarnished.

She could not help, behind the orderly and even-faced square seeing the mile of slum. She could not help, on turning aside suddenly from an elegant residential street, coming immediately on the rows of damp and stale-smelling public houses in their rows of damp and stale-smelling alleys. She saw the sour-smelling unkempt blowsy peacock-voiced women, the hollow-faced men unfitted for their work, the hordes of ill-clad pale children sitting for hours on the cold evil-smelling pavements. Unhealthy and rotten like soaked stumps of dead trees. She saw the hordes of mutilated beggars; heard the tuneless voices of myriad street singers; saw the stones covered with the ghostly trees and water-falls of a thousand pavement artists.

And was indifferent to none of it. (Lord! what then lies behind the eye of man that can so alter the perspective of his soul as to bring to the one courage and decision and to the next anger and futility?) What did the reverse side of the moon matter that she should be for ever trying to stuff it in her pocket? Was she not being unfair? Because streets were smoked out with petrol fumes and alive with motor horns where she remembered the tang of horse dung and the trimly beaten measure of slow-stepping carriage horses; or because, coming from years under a vast and luminous sky and colour and plenty and people strong in their work and with warm-baked skins and naked strongly planted children with backbones like ropes of vine knotted and unbreakable, she found the air thick and unpalatable and hung like a piece of sodden grey cloth above the opening between squares and streets. What right had she to question what she saw? What exactly did she want? A feeling of bitterness and impatience came over her, as to one who sees a favourite child doing mean and unworthy acts. What then would she advise? Nothing, nothing, said Ruth avoiding a black shape advancing toward her with a drunkard's amiable concentration.

She sought but found none of the appropriate emotions. All her life like a wish laid on her she had missed appropriate emotions. Even as a child, and in the teeth of protest, the cuckoo's song had seemed to her immeasurably superior to anything the nightingale could offer. And now she wanted, she tried, to see World-Trade and Hub of the Universe and London's teeming masses and London's great army of workers, and saw nothing but herded millions rushing to their daily death entangled in the puppet string of civilisation: hunger their fear, respectability their reward.

Yesterday in an underground train sitting opposite an elderly man with three separate strings of red hair drawn across his brow and turning the leaves of his newspaper with a thin green hand, she had thought of how a story could be written of just such an elderly man who had lived (like this) all his life underground, in trains to and from work, in badly lit offices, in badly ventilated badly designed houses, in the grave, and one day in a book or in his newspaper he read of the life and habits of the mole. And the absurd little creature (look! there was his picture, he pointed, for his son) made him laugh and laugh and laugh.

When the elderly man stood up and went out leaving his newspaper on the seat, she thought: now he has forgotten his armour. For it did seem to her that the people she saw about her carried their newspapers much as their ancestors carried a shield. In uniform self-defence, it seemed, they travelled in the trains and omnibuses with their heads wrapped in the daily papers. The great narcotic, the Universal Opiate for which the Londoner paid his daily tax to get himself out of embarrassment. Which protected his outward self on his way to work against any man or woman who dare approach or look at him. Which he clutched to protect his inner self from the fear of sudden doubt that in his daily grind from nine in the morning to six in the evening, he might not, after all who knows?, be doing a hard day's work; be pulling his weight in the world; be doing a man's work; the nation's work; the world's work.

And what more than anything was so sad about this dry-grin of humanity, she thought, was to see them all being so splendidly brave about nothing: about nothing at all.

Fear! How full of fear they were, the handful of people of leisurely and secluded lives gathered together as though for mutual protection in the pleasant quiet of Hans Crescent. That, too, was new to her. How it shocked one this sense of insecurity in people whose lives, concluded and unalterable, had never known the meaning of change or fear! It was as tangible a thing as the hopelessness of mean streets and the worry on the faces of people hurrying to their work. Fear and worry. They gave it off collectively as an aura.

Particularly the very ancient Lady Neuerheim with all the desolation of decay about her, making of her a tiresome old woman. She had long outstayed her welcome. She knew it. Her wealth and jewels stood for much. She knew that also. Apparently she belonged to one of those jewish diamond firms for whom the english took South Africa. She had once been fabulously wealthy. But times were not what they were. So she complained bitterly of supertax and death duties. A brave smile hovered; everyone seemed to be awaiting her death to take possession of her money. They visited her only to eat her food. She was upset to tears at a newspaper gossip paragraph mentioning the pictures and gems in her country-house collection. Every thief in Europe has read about me today! she smiled bravely through thick glasses. As evening came her fears lessened. The effort of outliving the crowded daylight hours over, and one more victory won from Time, she could rest. She would be seen, guided by a resigned and competent-looking companion-secretary up the long dining-room, her white hair rayed with jewels, jewels covering her yellowing hands and holding up her throat, and of course the renowned pearls, wound and rewound, and even so reaching almost to the hem of her skirt, as they appear in the Sargent portrait which she mentioned repeatedly.

—Ah Sargent! said Mrs Saffron Oake. I place them together: Sargent and Wagner. Two great souls inseparable. (And Siena. Ah Siena. Mrs Saffron Oake wished to die in Siena. Or when dead to be carried to Siena. But she must know Siena? Not know *Siena* after thirty years in Italy? Impossible not to know Siena. Everyone. Then just as soon as she returns she must visit Siena, said Mrs Saffron Oake, and tell her exactly what her first impressions were. Only the first impressions. All other impressions are useless, useless. I go by first impressions only; and they never fail me.)

But a nice woman. The least fearful of them all. (What need Mrs Saffron Oake fear while stands Siena?) Perfecting a technique of conversation which depended on asking questions and answering them herself; stampeding people into listening to her singing of *stornelli toscani* which, she delighted to recall, she had gathered herself during her Tuscan wanderings. A short lecture preceding each song. A Miss Templestone at the piano throws up a dust of notes. Mrs Saffron Oake thrusts her mouth in a protruding oval and from a hidden recess produces a sudden sound. Listening, marvelling, knowing that her approval is sought, that her twenty-two years in Italy are being evoked and sung to, puts down her coffee-cup, has not the heart, smiles, leans forward and applauds just so much more warmly than the rest. (I must be old, she thinks, admonishing herself. I have an old-womanish heart.) Mrs Saffron Oake smiles in her direction and is off and away producing more sounds from hidden recesses. But a nice woman, the least fearful of them all: having Siena.

Whereas Mrs Warburton Drury, not having Siena, but having three daughters "out" and not doing at all well (common knowledge) although at home in most of the houses that mattered, being related in varying degrees to all of them, and having been bridesmaids at any number of important weddings and being dowdy on enviable dress allowances, and the second girl talking everywhere of independence and earning one's own living these days: hated many things: miners out of work; anglo-catholics; jews; americans; fascists; that nasty-looking man Mussolini; the Labour Party; all people who had no Right to govern; and the modern tendency to regard marriage as a light and impermanent tie.

A Colonel Crispin Farr said: We should refuse to shake hands with the Russians until they apologise for killing the Tsar.

A Miss Bettine Ross who seemed to have neither artistic nor practical use, nodded vigorously.

A Major Farjeon Gorr wished to see every —— socialist hanged on Tower Hill with other blackguards such as Bernard Shaw and Trotsky; and would like to take the job on himself and see it well and properly done. (Why were elderly army men so blustering and bitter?)

A Miss Alberta Braithey turned her heavy autumnal face to the light and said to her, slowly and conclusively: I have never thought much of my face, you know. But there must be something in it as so many men have loved it.

—No, said Ruth replying to a direct question. I hardly agree. A million shorthand-typists remain a million shorthand-typists, but a million mothers can found a nation. The italian woman, as you say, is a born mother (though that is much a matter of olive oil and sunlight). The italian view of an englishwoman is an old maid who kisses cats and fondles dogs. The italian woman kicks the cat and beats the dog: but she caresses the child. It is much a matter of climate.

(—I nearly dayed of laughing, said Miss Templestone, later. To say a thing like that one must be made; quite made.)

—But *you*, said Joan Agnew rapturously. You're different. You're so original, you know. You're marvellous. And without trying, like all the rest of them. God, said Joan dabbing ungracefully with her cigarette ash, I wish I'd had you for a mother!

She was taking Joan to a play. The girl's version of herself was that she was sponging on a sister who had married money and had left a Shropshire vicarage with no intentions of returning until she hadn't a bean. So she was looking for a job. Did she know of one? Everybody works these days; all her friends were sharing lingerie or flower shops or being mannequins or "walking on" in revues or getting on the gossip pages of the daily papers. One must do *something* or life would be too damned dull.

Ruth liked her. She was shocked and impressed and amazed. This, then, was the modern girl the newspapers spoke so much about. Keen-eyed, fleshless, arrogant. She liked it. It was new to her. It had promise. Everywhere there was fear, a sense of danger, a sense of despair, a smell of decay: but the young women had a certain hard fleshless courage. They had promise. It was new to her and interesting.

On coming out of the theatre they saw a crowd gathered. From the hole in the centre came a small querulous voice: An' I don't want to die 'ere in the street. O my Gawd I don't want to die 'ere in the street. . . .

—What d'you make of it? said the girl placing her long elegant legs on the opposite seat as the taxi jerked forward.

She hoped that he would not have to die in the street, haunted by the simplicity of the man's appeal.

—I meant the play.

She went to too few plays to be a good judge. But she didn't like it. ·

—To me you all seem to be prying into other people's bedrooms. You have all an eye at the bedroom keyholes of the world. I don't like your idea of what you call sex. There is too much of it. It is an obsession or a disease. You turn love either into a wasting disease or a perpetual Chopin nocturne.

—Um, said the girl throwing a match out of the window. There's something in what you say. It is rather a dirty business. Tonight's papers say the Luff divorce cost over £50,000. Nasty, isn't it? As though it matters in whose bed one sleeps. . . .

There he glowed like mother-of-pearl in the strong sunlight! He stared back at her from stark blue-black eyes set in an incredibly blue face against an incredibly blue sky. She sat on the edge of the red-plush seat as she had sat on the edge of her bed that night in the Taverna, heavy with tears that would not be shed. Irresolute she sat, as a nun about to break her vows and unable to do so.

She knew that they were now valuable these tortured fierce-looking paintings which she had watched him at work upon and found so strange. And still found strange but for the grape-bloom glow on this child made of the earth he squatted on, and which she too had understood. Two thousand guineas for *The Modern Blue Boy,* as the newspapers called it: and a bargain, it appeared, bought from the Paris art dealers who had bought it directly from the artist for sixty pounds. He had asked one hundred.

A vagabond, a stranger to you! How little that had meant, then. How evenly the days had passed. How very simple things were. How little those who achieved it lived for posterity! She had gathered in the books about him. She could not recognise Uller in these pictures of him, any more than she could recognise her father in their pen-pictures of him. Those who came afterwards, in hearsay, in admiration, meant nothing: meant less than nothing. The stories of his life in Paris with Nasetkin were witty and amusing. Nasetkin was made much of to give colour to the rumour of their intimacy. His biographers puzzled and surmised about an italian woman he seemed to have met the year spent in Italy prior to the war. She was to be seen in several of his later canvases. In the large *Woman and Child* the naked child on her lap is again the Blue Boy. Was she the child's mother? At first: probably. Later: undoubtedly. A rather severe head, even-featured, serious, remote. It ran through his later sketches like a litany.

They were clever, condescending, awestruck. They made of him a braggart, overbearing, callous, which seemed to give him additional glamour in their eyes. They worshipped him from far as a form of human burning bush which none dared approach.

Sitting there staring at the blue distorted child she seemed to have been on a long journey and to be nearing home. Have I been a lonely woman? she asked. Have I repaid my debt? Or was there never a debt to repay but in her wilful mind?

Did it matter if one human creature more or less was born into the world crippled, insentient? It happened to the most honest people. People who loved their children. People who desired children; who waited for years; who hoped; made actual prayers. And then Nature played them just such a trick: sent them just such an answer. See, said Nature, see what I have reserved for you! But all that was beside the point. Without waiting, without wanting, she had played just such a trick on Nature. See, she had said, see what I am giving you! A line she had memorised from her lesson books as a child came back to her: *and the elephant said to the flea: don't push.*

What intricate, what appalling things one did with the few years of life given one! But *you,* you're different. And she had blushed. There was a novelty and a certain glamour about the new young woman: but was she altogether satisfying? Had she attained anything not previously attained? A certain independence and what she called self-expression. A following less efficiently and more loudly professions which men had followed for years as a matter of course. There was about her a look of impermanence difficult to classify. A look of today. Something momentary. She would grow old and leave the world exactly as she found it.

You, you're different! How often had that been held against her? How she herself had reproached this very difference, this difficulty to take for granted, to produce appropriate emotions on their appropriate occasions, leaving her lonely as an invert. For surely (she thought) it was a form of mental inversion this loneliness of hers among her fellow-creatures; her desolate belief only in the few and fear of the many; her lack of hope; her sense of the purposelessness of it all. But times change. Now one not only might but one was expected to be different. What they called being different had an especial social value. It acted on others as a charm. She was shocked. She could not understand. Now, it seemed, the emancipated woman wanted no children. Women kept their figures and their jobs; besides, motor-cars (said Joan) were less expensive. How monstrous! she thought, understanding not at all. How mean. She hurried away from the blue Giovann' in his setting of radiant sky. She would return, soon; but she must go now.

Outside a steely rain fell in long detached needles. In the wet deserted street a solitary policeman in a rain-lacquered cape stood staring at the river. It was cold and wet but she must walk, she felt. Grey and black and black and grey and again grey and again black. She passed through it all as through a cloud, seeing nothing but opaque grey and solid black. People lived in this solid black: breathed soaked-in this opaque grey. She passed through the squalor of Westminster. Narrow streets leading out of and into narrow streets, and on each the same cold and desolate face. A grey mould covered everything.

She walked on through her cloud. She was startled by the sudden thought that had she lived among it all these years she would have noticed nothing. A blue expanse of sky had done that for her. Times without number she would have been driven through such streets, less alive than the blind man in the doorway, cap in hand. (He spat on the coin and bit it. Why did he not wear his hat, and trust to his placard on such a day? People don't like it, he said. They likes a man to be cawld and ter look it, afor' they gives 'im anything. They likes ter see yer fair dyin' for their copper. Thenk yew kindly lidy. Thenk yew. Thenk yew.)

And he? What would he have become in the protected ease among those fortunate few who, like himself, were lifted above such desolate reality? Suddenly she saw him lying asleep in the shade of the rock on the hot yellow sand under a cloudless sky.

In Trafalgar Square a procession of unemployed was passing. Traffic was held up; the people waited. The men, it seemed, were from the distressed areas of the North; were from the closed steel and iron works; were miners from Wales; were dockers from the Clyde. They had gathered in the North and had come down on foot with their banners and their massed appeal to protest. The men were soaked and shivering. Their faces were a uniform grey and haggard and emptied of all expression save hunger and weariness. Their heads drooped forward on their necks. They shuffled past, unsubstantial as ghosts. At intervals mounted police in lacquered capes rode beside them, but paying scarce attention to them, so worn and spiritless they were.

Again she had a sight of him lying in the shade of the rock on the hot yellow sand under a blue outstretched sky. How she had feared him! How long now, she wondered, had she feared him, imagining his reproach? What then was the more culpable: physical or mental insentience? To be unable to understand or to refuse? She thought of the squalor, the grey faces, of blind men standing with uncovered heads because others liked to see them cold, of the dreariness of poverty, the dreariness of gentility, the limited outlook of the one, the limited outlook of the other, the decaying world closing in on the new life, and everywhere people being so splendidly brave about nothing, about nothing at all. What could she, she asked, what could she have told him?

There was a movement and sudden noise and a sound of angry voices. A policeman was speaking to one of the men. The man answered. The policeman made a menacing movement with his arm. He was threatening to strike the man. To her surprise she began to tremble; she was not certain but had the impression that her teeth were chattering. He must not strike, she thought. She must cry out. It could not be that such a wraith of a man, such a grey hollow thing, should be struck a blow, a well-fed hearty blow, for a mere interchange of words. The people around, those standing near him, she thought foolishly, would not allow it. At last the policeman relaxed his arm. He shouted something at the man. The man cursed under his breath, as the policeman turned away. She ceased trembling.

Perhaps, she thought, if they could accept death this collective fear, this smell of decay, would leave them. How clean (she thought) how final death. To have lived and to die. How complete, how wise the man (she thought) who having lived can meet death carelessly, knowing it final. She remembered how worn and tired the earth looks after the harvest and before the winter sleep; and with what zest the trees and vines flung off their brown and brittle leaves. And then remembered the musty fruit on barrows, or scarce and unvaried behind plate glass, which those who sold had done nothing to produce. She thought of Andrea balanced on his heels, tilting the jug of yellow-clouded wine. She saw again the market place in Florence. The earth: with what dignity it invested man! With what generosity it repaid him his efforts in its service. Perhaps she had lived too long among peasants to be patient with the town dweller. Allow them no heaven, she thought. Dreaming away their lives in the expectation of living another. How much happier those (she thought) deprived of the mirage of a heaven, and living one life and living it fully.

On and on the procession shuffled, the men a uniform grey, haggard and emptied of all expression save hunger and weariness. Unsubstantial as ghosts they shuffled wanly past. The traffic held up: the people waiting.

In the growing press of people gathered there to attend this grotesque Calvary, she stood tearless and detached watching humanity carrying its Cross: bent, beaten and anxious, and yet more innocent than Christ. She turned to the group nearest her on the pavement; warmly dressed, middle-class. The man looked carved: the woman dried: the child bled: the dog inflated.

She turned away, again wondering what she could have told him. But now she smiled. She no longer reproached herself.

Although Olive Moore's four published books constitute a remarkable achievement, placing her among the best British novelists of the twentieth century, she is virtually unknown to literary historians. She isn't listed in any of the encyclopedias of women writers that have appeared recently, nor is she mentioned in any of the many books on modern British literature we've consulted. The only reference book that does take note of her is *Authors Today and Yesterday* (an early version of the now-standard *Twentieth Century Authors*), for which Moore furnished this autobiographical sketch in 1933:

I was born in Hereford, on the border of Wales, which in my childhood used to upset me greatly as I felt London, or Rome, or Ancient Greece, or something really grandiose was the only place to be born in. I was sent abroad to a Convent at the age of five; I suppose I learned to read and write; a great war broke out, which meant less than nothing to me, except that now I realise how fortunate I was to escape mob educational methods by which the brains and digestive organs of millions of small children are still being ruined daily. Since growing up, and of my own free will, I have studied art in Italy, and subjects which interested me, such as literature and language, at the Sorbonne.

My life is so completely dull and uneventful, that there is absolutely nothing to tell you about it. O yes. I was in New York November 1929–May 1930. Memorable to me—indeed unforgettable—because it was there that the MS of my book *Spleen* (Harper's published it as *Repentance at Leisure*) was burnt out in a hotel fire. Together with every garment I possessed, except an aged mackintosh in which I had been walking round Central Park in the rain. But *Spleen.* I would like to be stoical and exalted about it; but I cannot; it was an unhappy and deadly experience. I sat down and re-wrote it. Fortunately my prose is such that I have to write very slowly. I spend days reducing 500 words to 50. I loathe the easy and the slip-shod. So in a sense I memorise as I go along. I know some passages in my books word for word, because of this passion for simplifying. I remembered a great deal of *Spleen,* the rhythm, the construction. At least I can see that *now.* But *then,* it was torture. I don't know why I re-wrote it. I used to say that if I'd had a few pounds a week of my own, I'd never have touched a pen again. But I didn't have; so perhaps it was just as well.

But that wasn't my first book, which was *Celestial Seraglio: A Tale of Convent Life.* Appeared 1929, October. England only. *Spleen* in November 1930.

Fugue, March 1932. A limited edition, signed and numbered, of an essay on D. H. Lawrence (published by C. Lahr, the Blue Moon Press, London) *Further Reflections on the Death of a Porcupine,* came out November 1932. I shall be re-publishing it in a book of essays this autumn or early next year.

There is little to tell you, or that matters, about me. I am by nature solitary and contemplative, very happy, very morose. I loathe books and never read them. Except informative books, giving me facts, any facts and all facts. I love travel best of all, and yet get very impatient with it. I like walking. I like talking. I love meeting people once. I love best knowing absolutely no one; but watching every one. I dislike having to live in London, a parochial little village. But I have to. I dislike it so much, that it does me (creatively) an awful lot of good. It's the pearl in my oyster. I dislike things very thoroughly indeed. I like disliking them. Otherwise (I live in London, Eng.) one gets genteel, tea shoppe, bored, refined, amateurish. All things which make it so difficult for the creative artist to live in England, which is secure, pleasant, imitative, watery. But fortunately I never meet people, and so am saved from contamination.

I have no sense of hero-worship. I respect all men who are master of their jobs; I say men, meaning men. I don't believe in women. They seem able to do everything but think. Yet they get away with it.

I believe only in the conscious artist. I would wish my work to be judged on the texture of my thought and the disposition of my sentences.

This provocative sketch was reprinted (slightly abridged) in the 1942 edition of *Twentieth Century Authors,* where a few more facts are given by the editor:

Her *Amazon and Hero: The Drama of the Greek War for Independence,* on which she has been at work since 1931, has not yet been published. There is no recent word of her, in an England which she can no longer describe as "secure, pleasant, imitative, watery." She is unmarried, and though she does not give her birthdate, it was probably about 1905.

No further documentary evidence is available; there is no indication that *Amazon and Hero* was ever published, nor has any obituary been found.

A request for further information in the *Times Literary Supplement* elicited a reply from David Goodway of the University of Leeds, who informed us that "Olive Moore" was actually a pseudonym for Constance Vaughan and that she "is almost certainly dead (and died before 1970 or thereabouts)." Prof. Goodway also noted that "Connie" Vaughan was part of Charles Lahr's Red Lion Street circle, a literary group that gravitated towards a bookstore specializing in radical literature located at 68 Red Lion Street, Holborn. The proprietor, Charles Lahr, published literary pamphlets as well, including stories by such writers as D. H. Lawrence, T. F. Powys, Rhys Davies, and, as she notes in her sketch, Moore's essay on Lawrence. (See David Goodway, "Charles Lahr: Anarchist, Bookseller, Publisher," *London Magazine*, June/July 1977, 46-55.) Lahr also published occasional Christmas cards consisting of short verses by some of his writers. Moore contributed one for Christmas 1932, one of a set of six signed copies of poems by various authors; hers is entitled "Statement" and was reprinted in *The Apple Is Bitten Again*, as was her Lawrence essay (pp. 371 and 394-402, respectively, in her *Collected Writings*).

Alec Bristow, one of the few surviving members of the Red Lion Street circle, wrote us an informative letter that is worth quoting at length; regretting that he didn't know when she died (or even that she was dead), he explained:

We had completely lost touch many years ago, though in the early thirties we spent a good deal of time together. I have no letters from her either; we both lived in Bloomsbury (she in Doughty Street and I in Mecklenburgh Street), only a couple of minutes' walk from each other, so we had no need to correspond by letter when it was so easy to visit.

We first met at Charles Lahr's bookshop in Red Lion Street, which was a focal point in Bloomsbury for writers to meet each other. I had reviewed O.M.'s novel *Fugue* very favourably in a literary-cum-political publication of the day called the *Twentieth Century*, and she had expressed to Charles a wish to meet me, which he arranged. We soon became friends, sharing as we did similar likes and (particularly) dislikes.

She gave me copies of her other two novels, which I still have. The first, *Celestial Seraglio*, was of course largely autobiographical, and she confessed to me that the character Mavis was very much a self-portrait. The second, *Spleen*, was much more a novel of ideas; the title, she told me, was inspired by the poem sequence "Spleen et Idéal" in *Les Fleurs du Mal* by Charles Baudelaire, whose work she greatly admired. Indeed, she gave me her copies, which I have still, of both *Les Fleurs du Mal* and *La Vie Douloureuse de Charles Baudelaire*, on the title page of which she had written in her tiny writing "Olive Moore, Bruxelles 1929"—so she must by then have given herself the pseudonym under which her books were published during the next few years.

Her real name, as you know, was Constance Vaughan. She was known as Connie by her colleagues at the *Daily Sketch*, a (long defunct) newspaper where she worked as a journalist. I never called her anything but Olive, since she made it clear that she much preferred that name. She once told me that the reason why she had chosen her pseudonym was that Olive represented an acquired taste, dry and sophisticated, and Moore suggested that once the taste had been acquired her readers would want more.

Our conversations were almost entirely about books and writing. She hardly ever referred to her background and upbringing, which she clearly wanted to forget. I did, however, have the impression that her parents had separated, like those of Mavis in *Celestial Seraglio,* and that she had preferred her father to her mother—who, she told me in passing, had once called her a monster. I do not know what other personal ties, if any, she had at the time we knew each other, though I believe she had had an affair with Sava Botzaris, whose fierce-looking sculpture of her appears as the frontispiece to *The Apple Is Bitten Again,* the last of her books to be published, as far as I am aware.

We had used the same portrait in *Further Reflections on the Death of a Porcupine,* which first appeared in 1933 in a limited edition of 99 copies, published by the Blue Moon Press, of which I was then chairman, in partnership with Charles Lahr. The way it happened is that O.M. told me that she had written an essay on D. H. Lawrence but thought it unsuitable for Jarrolds, who had published her novels but were not in the field of *belles lettres.* I said I would finance a limited edition, and I wrote the prospectus for it (signed A.B. because Olive did not want people to think she had written her own blurb). To the best of my recollection all the copies were sold and I nearly recouped the money I had paid. We hit on the title not only because Lawrence had published an essay entitled *Reflections on the Death of a Porcupine* but because he had been rather a prickly character himself.

It was in acknowledgment of my role in getting the book published that my copy is inscribed "To Alec Bristow, who is responsible for this—Olive Moore." Later, of course, *Further Reflections* was included in full in her collection of *pensées* entitled *The Apple Is Bitten Again,* published by Wishart & Co—who, like Jarrolds and the Blue Moon Press, ceased to exist many years ago.

The highly stylised portrait sculpture by Sava Botzaris does not give me a satisfactory impression of the O.M. that I knew—except perhaps for the somewhat intimidating air which she could convey to people who bored her. Though of medium height and unremarkable features and build, she certainly made her presence felt in any company. Dining with her in a restaurant was quite an experience; her carrying voice and penetrating laugh would make the glasses ring and other diners look round. . . .

You are, I am sure, quite correct in assuming that her projected book *Amazon and Hero* was never published. I very much doubt whether she ever finished it; she had started making notes for it when I knew her, but I think she was finding the prospect of doing the necessary research rather daunting, quite apart from the labour of the actual writing. Her style may be easy to read, but being a perfectionist she found it agony to write.

Aside from the fact that she was acquainted with the Scottish poet Hugh MacDiarmid, nothing further is known of Olive Moore at this time. Anyone knowing more is encouraged to write to the Publisher.

A Note on the Text

The text reprinted here is the one established for Dalkey Archive's edition of Moore's *Collected Writings* (1992). *Spleen* was first published in the U.S. by Harper & Brothers in October 1930 (under the singularly inappropriate title *Repentance at Leisure*) and the following month in England by Jarrolds (under the title *Spleen*, as the author always referred to it). There is every indication that the U.S. edition is closer to Moore's manuscript than the British edition, and for that reason we have used it as our text. Some of these indications are spaces between paragraphs (where the British edition closes them up, causing some confusion when the last line of a paragraph ends flush right); the absence of periods after such abbreviations as Mrs and Dr; at least one instance where a word is missing from the British edition, which suggests that the American edition was set from a manuscript rather than from the British edition; and numerous indications in the British edition of the hand of a conventionally minded copy-editor: inserting many correct but unnecessary commas, capitalizing nationalities that Moore apparently preferred in lower-case, and correcting a few errors. Only these corrections and the title *Spleen* have been used from the British edition, since this seems to be the title Moore preferred.

One uniform departure from the original has been made throughout this text: it was Moore's habit to begin each new paragraph flush left with a one-line space separating it from the previous one. We find this wasteful and aesthetically displeasing, especially with exchanges of dialogue and one-sentence paragraphs; consequently, paragraphs are indicated in the standard manner: indented and closed-up. Otherwise, we follow Moore's text faithfully, retaining her old-fashioned orthography, British spelling, and occasional eccentricities. (In *Spleen*, nationalities like English and Italian are not capitalized.) Typos and various inconsistencies in the treatment of words have been silently corrected.

DALKEY ARCHIVE PAPERBACKS

DALKEY ARCHIVE PAPERBACKS

ZUKOFSKY, LOUIS. *Collected Fiction* — 9.95
ZWIREN, SCOTT. *God Head* — 10.95

FICTION: BRITISH

BROOKE-ROSE, CHRISTINE. *Amalgamemnon* — 9.95
CHARTERIS, HUGO. *The Tide Is Right* — 9.95
FIRBANK, RONALD. *Complete Short Stories* — 9.95
GALLOWAY, JANICE. *Foreign Parts* — 12.95
GALLOWAY, JANICE. *The Trick Is to Keep Breathing* — 11.95
HUXLEY, ALDOUS. *Point Counter Point* — 13.95
MOORE, OLIVE. *Spleen* — 10.95
MOSLEY, NICHOLAS. *Accident* — 9.95
MOSLEY, NICHOLAS. *Impossible Object* — 9.95
MOSLEY, NICHOLAS. *Judith* — 10.95
MOSLEY, NICHOLAS. *Natalie Natalia* — 12.95

FICTION: FRENCH

BUTOR, MICHEL. *Portrait of the Artist as a Young Ape* — 10.95
CÉLINE, LOUIS-FERDINAND. *North* — 13.95
CREVEL, RENÉ. *Putting My Foot in It* — 9.95
ERNAUX, ANNIE. *Cleaned Out* — 10.95
GRAINVILLE, PATRICK. *The Cave of Heaven* — 10.95
NAVARRE, YVES. *Our Share of Time* — 9.95
QUENEAU, RAYMOND. *The Last Days* — 11.95
QUENEAU, RAYMOND. *Pierrot Mon Ami* — 9.95
ROUBAUD, JACQUES. *The Great Fire of London* — 12.95
ROUBAUD, JACQUES. *The Plurality of Worlds of Lewis* — 9.95
ROUBAUD, JACQUES. *The Princess Hoppy* — 9.95
SIMON, CLAUDE. *The Invitation* — 9.95

FICTION: GERMAN

SCHMIDT, ARNO. *Collected Stories* — 13.50
SCHMIDT, ARNO. *Nobodaddy's Children* — 13.95

FICTION: IRISH

CUSACK, RALPH. *Cadenza* — 7.95
MAC LOCHLAINN, ALF. *The Corpus in the Library* — 11.95
MACLOCHLAINN, ALF. *Out of Focus* — 5.95
O'BRIEN, FLANN. *The Dalkey Archive* — 9.95

DALKEY ARCHIVE PAPERBACKS

O'BRIEN, FLANN. *The Hard Life*   11.95
O'BRIEN, FLANN. *The Poor Mouth*   10.95

FICTION: LATIN AMERICAN AND SPANISH

CAMPOS, JULIETA. *The Fear of Losing Eurydice*   8.95
LINS, OSMAN. *The Queen of the Prisons of Greece*   12.95
PASO, FERNANDO DEL. *Palinuro of Mexico*   14.95
RÍOS, JULIÁN. *Poundemonium*   13.50
SARDUY, SEVERO. *Cobra* and *Maitreya*   13.95
TUSQUETS, ESTHER. *Stranded*   9.95
VALENZUELA, LUISA. *He Who Searches*   8.00

POETRY

ANSEN, ALAN. *Contact Highs: Selected Poems 1957-1987*   11.95
BURNS, GERALD. *Shorter Poems*   9.95
FAIRBANKS, LAUREN. *Muzzle Thyself*   9.95
GISCOMBE, C. S. *Here*   9.95
MARKSON, DAVID. *Collected Poems*   9.95
THEROUX, ALEXANDER. *The Lollipop Trollops*   10.95

NONFICTION

FORD, FORD MADOX. *The March of Literature*   16.95
GREEN, GEOFFREY, ET AL. *The Vineland Papers*   14.95
MATHEWS, HARRY. *20 Lines a Day*   8.95
MOORE, STEVEN. *Ronald Firbank: An Annotated Bibliography*   30.00
ROUDIEZ, LEON S. *French Fiction Revisited*   14.95
SHKLOVSKY, VIKTOR. *Theory of Prose*   14.95
WEST, PAUL. *Words for a Deaf Daughter* and *Gala*   12.95
WYLIE, PHILIP. *Generation of Vipers*   13.95
YOUNG, MARGUERITE. *Angel in the Forest*   13.95

For a complete catalog of our titles, write to Dalkey Archive Press,
Illinois State University, Campus Box 4241, Normal, IL 61790-4241,
fax (309) 438-7422, or visit the Dalkey Archive Press website at
http://www.cas.ilstu.edu/english/dalkey/dalkey.html